THE BIG
DOG CAPER

THE BIG DOG CAPER

BLAKE NELSON

ISBN: Softcover   978-1-5245-3648-0
            eBook   978-1-5245-3647-3

Print information available on the last page.

Rev. date: 08/19/2016

To order additional copies of this book, contact:
Xlibris
1-888-795-4274
www.Xlibris.com
Orders@Xlibris.com
748093

TABLE OF CONTENTS

CHAPTER

A dog barks at 4:30 in the morning. Captain Randy Miller wakes up and looks at the clock radio. Then he sits up, puts on his glasses and gets out of bed. He walks over to the bedroom window and looks outside. He sees nothing, then looks down at his wife Elaine. He wonders how she can sleep through the racket? He takes another look out the window, still nothing.

Realizing he has to get up in a couple hours for his New York/ London flight, he walks back to his bed. He takes off his glasses and gets back into bed. He falls asleep right away and doesn't wake up till the clock radio goes off.

At 6:30 in the morning the clock radio goes off. Randy turns it off and gets out of bed. He walks into the bathroom and gets ready to take a shower. Elaine wakes up shortly after that and puts on her bathrobe. She walks downstairs to the kitchen to make breakfast for the family. She decides to make pancakes, bacon, eggs, and toast for breakfast.

While she starts cooking her 2 boys wake up and walks into the kitchen. Mark (the oldest) says, "Good morning mom." Elaine then turns around and says, "Good morning Mark." Mark then jabs his younger brother Scott in the ribs with his right elbow. "Oh yeah, good morning mom." Elaine smiles and says, "good morning to you too Scott." Elaine then turns back to her cooking and tells her boys to go play in the playroom and that she will call for them later.

Randy then walks downstairs wearing his pilots uniform and enters the kitchen. Kisses his wife and says, "good morning dear." Elaine then smiles and asks her husband if he slept well? Randy answered and said, "I woke up at 4:30 because of some barking dog."

"I'm sorry to hear that. Any idea who's dog it was?" Replied Elaine. "At first I wasn't sure, but now I think it might have been Buster, the Hanson's German Shepherd.", answered Randy. "That's odd, he normally sleeps through the night, nothing wakes him up.", replied Elaine.

The phone then rings and Elaine answers, "Hello........Joyce you are going to have to calm down......Buster's missing?" Randy looks concerned. "Well, if we see Buster we will let you know......o.k. good bye." Elaine then hung up the phone and turned to her husband Randy. "That was Joyce Hanson, she says Buster is missing."

"Did they call the police?", asked Randy. Elaine paused for a few seconds, then said, "she's calling them now." Randy thinks for a moment then asks, "I wonder who would kidnap a dog and why would they do that?" Elaine turns and resumes cooking breakfast. "Go and tell the boys breakfast will be ready in a couple of minutes.", said Elaine. "Where are they?", asked Randy. "In the playroom.", replied Elaine. Randy then turns and leaves the kitchen and heads off for the playroom.

When Randy arrived in the playroom, he found the 2 boys fighting over a toy firetruck. "boys!", yelled Randy. "why are you guys fighting?" The boys quit fighting and Mark looked up at his father and said, "sorry dad." Then Scott looked at his dad and said, "I was playing with the firetruck first and Mark took it from me.", Randy took a deep breath and said, "now Scott, what did I tell you about sharing?", Scott looked down at the floor for a second then looked back at Randy and replied, "I'll try to remember that next time.", "That's better", replied Randy, "now put away your toys and come to breakfast."

The boys and Randy sat down at the table and Elaine started to put food on the table. After she was done, then she sat down and they started eating.

Elaine looked at her husband and asked, "what time is your flight deer?", "9:00 a.m." answered Randy. "Hey dad, are you getting us souvenir hats like the ones the guards at Buckingham Palace wear?" Randy smiles and says, "of course Mark." Randy then looks at his watch and realizes he has to leave in 5 minutes. "Look at the time, I've got to leave shortly." Elaine then asks, "do you have time to finish breakfast?" Randy thinks for a moment and answers, "most of it."

"Now you boys behave for your mother while I'm gone." Mark and Scott look up at their dad and say, "yes dad." Randy eats a little more food, then stands up and says, "I better get going." He leaves the table and runs upstairs. Everyone else continues eating. "Mom can we go to the movies today?", asks Scott. "We'll see.", answered Elaine.

Randy walks downstairs with a small suitcase, sets it down on the floor and walks to the table. He kisses the boys on the forehead and Elaine on the lips. "Bye everyone, see you in a few days." He turns and makes his way to the front door picking up his suitcase on the way out.

"Do you boys have any plans for the day?", asked Elaine. "We're planning to hang out at Josh and Tyler Hanson's house", answered Mark. "Just so you know, Buster was kidnapped early this morning." The boys looked very shocked. "Who did it?" asked Scott. Elaine took a deep breath and replied, "we don't know yet, the police are going to be looking into it shortly." Mark looks down for a moment then back at his mom. "Are Josh and Tyler o.k.?" Elaine thinks for a short while and answers, "it would be best that you 2 don't talk about Buster being kidnapped in front of the Hanson's."

Mark and Scott finish breakfast, get up, and start to walk away. "You boys take a good shower and get dressed, then you can go out and play." "O.k." replied Mark. The boys then leave.

Elaine starts to clear the dishes from the kitchen table. As she is putting the dishes in the sink, she hears a police car drive by. She runs to the living room window and looks out. She sees the police car drive by on the way to the Hanson's house. She thinks to herself, "I bet they're going to investigate Buster's kidnapping." She walks back to the kitchen sink and starts washing the dishes.

After Elaine finishes washing the dishes, the boys run downstairs. "Bye mom." Yell both of the boys and they run out the door before she has a chance to say good bye to them. She thinks to herself, "they need to slow down." She walks into the living room, picks up a magazine and begins to read.

CHAPTER

Mark and Scott start walking toward the Hanson's house. They see the police car parked in the driveway. Joyce and the police are standing in the front lawn talking. Her 3-year-old daughter Kimberly is walking around near bye. Her sons Josh and Tyler are sitting on the front steps looking sad. Her husband David had just left for work.

Mark and Scott arrive and walk strait to where Josh and Tyler are sitting. They sit down right next to the Hanson boys. Josh takes a short breath and says, "this is a sad day for us." Scott looks down at the ground then back up and says, "we know." Josh sighs then says, "If I find who kidnapped Buster, I'm going to strangle him." The rest of the boys nod their heads in agreement.

Joyce then decides to show the cops the back yard where Buster was taken from. They walk to the gate and she shows them the broken pad lock. It is obvious to all that someone used forced entry. Then they walk to Buster's dog house. "This is where Buster sleeps most of the time.", said Joyce. The cops take a closer look at the dog house. One cop notices that whoever took Buster did a good job covering up evidence of a kidnapping.

The first cop asks Joyce if she knows anyone that might want to take him. Joyce thinks for a moment and says, "no one I can think of." The 2nd cop then says, "How about anyone in the neighborhood with a bad reputation?" Joyce thinks for a few seconds and says, "There is Kyle Smith who lives across the street. He just got out of juvenile detention and he's known as the neighborhood bully."

Back on the front steps the steps the boys talk about going to the park. Scott gets a look of excitement on his face and says, "hey, let's go to the park." The other boys looked puzzled. "Huh?", said Mark. Scott answers, "we can go to the park, that will help take our minds off of Buster for a while." Mark then replies, "that's a great idea Scott."

Joyce and the 2 police officers walk back into the front yard. Tyler yells out to her, "hey mom, we're going to the park." The boys get up and start walking. Joyce looks over to the boys and says, "make sure you're back here at noon for lunch." As they are walking by her Josh says to her, "we will."

As the boys walk off, the cops continue to talk to Joyce. The first police officer says, "we will go across the street and ask Kyle a few questions." Joyce shakes hands with the 2 officers and says, "thanks for coming." The officers leave and Joyce walks back into the house. While the police officers are walking across the street, the 2nd police officer says to the 1st, "Kyle isn't going to like seeing me again." The 1st officer then asks, "why is that?" The 2nd officer replies, "I'm the one that arrested him for breaking and entering."

The 2 cops show up at the Smith house and knock on the door. Some on looking neighbors think to themselves, "good lord, what has he done now?" The cops ring the doorbell and pound on the door a few times. After about a minute, Kyle opens the door. He is then standing in his pajamas and messy hair looking like he just woke up. He asks, "what do you pigs want?" He yawns and then the 1st cop answers, "are you aware that Buster from across the street has been kidnapped?"

"No, and I didn't do anything.", answered Kyle. The 1st cop then replies, "we would like to search the house, to verify that you're telling the truth." Kyle steps a side and says, "go right ahead, I've got nothing to hide."

Meanwhile at the park, Josh, Tyler, Mark, and Scott arrive to find a couple boys fighting with other kids (mostly boys) circled around them watching and cheering. Josh says, "let's go see this." The 4 boys run to where the fight is taking place. When they get there, they find one boy sitting on the other boy's stomach. He has the other boy's arms pinned under his knees. The boy on top is then punching the boy on the bottom, several times to the jaw and his right eye.

The boy on the bottom then yells, "all right, I give! I give!" The boy on top then gets up and raises his arms in victory. "Ha ha, I knew I'd kick your ass." The boy on the bottom is still lying on the ground crying. He then cries out, "you bastard!" The boy who won smiles and says, "whatever, you wimp." Then he walks off.

Josh, Tyler, Mark, and Scott then walk over to the playground equipment and start playing. Josh then asks, "I wonder what that was about?" Mark thinks for a moment and says, "who knows." Scott Looks at Josh and asks, do you think that kid who won can beat up Kyle?" Josh then answers, "I don't know, I guess." Scott replies, "it would be cool to see someone beat Kyle up."

Back at the Smith house, the cops are searching for anything that could prove Kyle kidnapped Buster. After about 15 minutes of searching, they found nothing. The first cop then says, "I guess you're clean." Kyle the replies, "see, I told you I didn't do anything." The 1st cop looks at Kyle and says, "we're sorry to bother you." The 2nd cop then asks, "by the way, where are your parents?" Kyle wishing, they would leave answers, "they both left for work about a half hour before you got here." The 2nd cop questions him, "they trust you home alone?" Kyle replies, "yeah, they think I'm old enough." The 2nd cop thinks for a moment then says, "we won't keep you any longer, we will go ahead and leave."

As the boys are walking back to the Hanson house, they notice the cops walking out of Kyle Smith's house. "Hey look", said Mark, "Deerfield, Illinois police coming out of Kyle's house." The cops walk up to the boys and the first cop asks them, "can we talk to you guys for a moment?" "I guess so" answered Josh. "We're looking for anyone who might have seen or heard anything relating to the kidnapping of Buster."

"I'm not sure, but I think my dad heard something.", said Mark. Cop 2 then asked, "where is your dad now?", Mark replied, "he's on his way to London, he'll probably call when he gets there." Cop 2 hands Mark a card and tells him to have his dad call him at the number on the card. Mark assures the cops that his dad will call. The cops then get in their car and drive off.

The boys walk into the back yard of the Hanson's house. They decide to sit down at the picnic table. Then Josh says, "for a while I thought Kyle was in trouble again." Scott then replies, "yeah, he sure gets into a lot of trouble these days." Josh then looks over at Scott and says, "I know his record all too well, with in the last 2 years he got 9 detentions, 3 suspensions, and almost got expelled." Tyler then added, "don't forget, he just got out of juvenile detention for breaking in and entering." Josh then added, "plus I think he was also charged with vandalism."

CHAPTER

3

Randy looks at his watch for a moment then at his co-pilot and says, "would like another coffee before we descend into London?" Co-pilot Mike thinks for a moment and says, "yeah sure." Randy then turns on the switch that calls the flight attendants. The head flight attendant, Susan then walks into the cockpit.

Susan then asks Randy and Mike if they want some more coffee. Mike then answers, "black for me." Randy then looks back at Susan and says, "cream for me." Susan then smiles and says, "coming right up guys." Then leaves.

Randy then stretches out his arms and yawns. Then he says to Mike, "these long overseas flights can really ware you out." Mike the nods his head and says, "I know what you mean." Randy then yawns one more time and says, "that coffee should help."

Susan returns with the coffee; hands Mike his coffee first then hands Randy his. Randy and Mike both thank Susan for their coffee and then she leaves. Mike takes one sip of his coffee and says, "great coffee as always." Randy sips his coffee, sets it down and says, "like always, Susan puts just the right amount of cream in mine."

Randy looks at the control panel and says, "we better start our descent into London." Randy and mike grab am hold of the controls and the air plane starts to descend. Randy turns on the cabin p.a. microphone on and says, "this is captain Miller of flight 1385 service to London. We have started our descent into London, at this time we ask you to please fasten your seatbelts and we thank you for flying with Trans-Atlantic Airlines."

A gust of wind shakes the plane for a moment. "Wow! That was unexpected", says Mike. Randy calls air traffic control on the radio to see if there are any storms in the area. They reply that there aren't any. "We shouldn't have more trouble", says Randy. He then takes a look at the controls and says to Mike, "let's get ready just in case."

Air traffic control reports that they are clear for landing and Randy lowers landing gear. They bring the plane down for a smooth landing and put on the brakes. Randy looks at Mike and says, "looks like another successful flight." He then turns on the cabin microphone and gives flight attendants and passengers final instructions.

After arriving at the gate the passengers and crew get off. Randy thinks to himself, "I got to call Elaine." He takes the plane to the hanger and gets out. Mike and Randy shake hands and say goodnight to each other. Carrying his suitcase through the airport, he catches cab and goes to the hotel.

Randy walked into the hotel looking groggy. He walks up to the front desk in the lobby and shows the clerk his confirmation number. She enters that number in the computer and says, "o.k. Randy, you'll be staying in room 135." Hands him the key. He thanks her and heads off to his room.

He enters the room, turns on the lights, and closes the door behind him. He spots the phone sitting on a table in the room and walks over there and sits down. Then he sets his suitcase down next to him. He picks up the phone and dials his home number.

Elaine answers the phone at home, "hello." She smiles when she hears her husband's voice, then she says, "oh honey it's so nice to hear you." Randy tells Elaine he arrived safely. Then Elaine covers up the mouthpiece of the phone and hollers, "boys, get down here! Your father's on the phone!"

The boys run downstairs in about 5 seconds. "So how's the weather in London?", asks Elaine. She smiles while listening to him. "O.k. the boys are her and they want to talk to you." Elaine hands the phone to Mark.

Mark picks up the phone and says, "hello dad." He listens to his dad talk for a moment, then says, "the cops were at Hanson's earlier

today. One of them gave me a card and asked me to have you call him."
Randy wondered and asked Mark what he wanted. Mark answered,
"they want to know if you seen or heard anything relating to Buster's
disappearance." Mark listens to his dad for a short while and asks,
"do you want the number?" "yes", replied Randy. Mark gives Randy
the phone number and says, "now here's Scott." Then hands Scott the
phone.

Scott picks up the phone and talks, "hello dad." Scott listens to his
dad talk for a while. Then says, "how's the weather in London?" Randy
tells Scott the weather is fair, but he is feeling tired from his flight. Scott
then asks, "Are we still getting those guard hats?" Randy then answers,
"if I find a store that sells them." Scott looks at his mom and says, "I
think mom wants to talk to you now." Scott hands the phone off to
Elaine and walks off.

Mark says to Scott quietly, "I think mom wants to make lovey dovey
talk to dad. Let's go play outside." They walk out to the back yard and
sit on the swings. "What do you think they want to talk about?", asked
Scott. "grown up things we're too young to understand.", replied Mark.

Mark and Scott start to swing back and forth. Scot then says, "let's
have a jumping off the swing contest." Mark answers, "you're on." The
boys then start swing high. Scott takes the first jump and goes about 4
feet. "beat that!", yells Scott. "I bet I can.", replied Mark. Mark takes a
jump and goes about 4 feet 3 inches. Then Mark says, "ha! I beat you!"
Elaine opens a window and yells, "boys come in for dinner!" Mark and
Scott run into the house.

Meanwhile, back in London, Randy dials the phone number to the
cop that had some questions for him. The phone rings 4 times and the
answering machine picks up. Randy leaves the following message, "this
is Captain Randy Miller, my son Mark told me to call you regarding
Buster's disappearance. It's probably after hours there for you, so I will
try again in the morning your time tomorrow." Then he hangs up.

Realizing how late it is, Randy decides to get ready for bed. He gets
out his pajamas from his suitcase and changes into them. Then grabs
his tooth brush and goes in the bathroom to brush his teeth. He thinks
for a moment as to what the cops might want to him about, then turns
out the lights and goes to bed.

The next morning Randy wakes and starts thinking about those
guard hats he promised his sons. He takes a shower and gets ready to

go shopping. After getting dressed he leaves his room and goes to the dining room for breakfast.

In the dining room, he grabs a plate and puts on it, eggs, bacon, and a couple pancakes. He picks up a copy of the local newspaper and starts to read while eating. He reads a news story about 3 guys who were murdered by some guy with an axe. He thinks to himself, "dear God, no!"

After reading about the axe murder, he puts down the newspaper and finishes breakfast. He walks out of the dining room and heads to the front desk. Randy spots a young lady sitting at the front desk. He asks her if she knows of any place that sells souvenir guard hats. She writes down the names and addresses of 4 places and tells him 1 of these might. He grabs the sheet of paper, thanks her and heads out the door.

Randy signals for a taxi cab and gets one right away. He instructs the driver to take him to the 1st store on his list. On the way there, the driver asks him, "would you mind if I turn on the radio?" Randy thinks for a second and says, "go ahead." The driver then turns on the radio and the announcer says, "the police are still looking for a suspect in the axe killer case."

Randy says, "I read about that in the paper this morning, I hope they find who did it." The driver looks in his rearview mirror and says, "they've been trying to solve that case for the last couple of days." Randy thinks for a few seconds and says, "maybe a clue will show up today."

After about 5 minutes the driver stops the car at the store. Then he says, "this is the place you wanted." Randy pays his fare and says, "thanks for the ride." Then he gets out and the driver drives off. Randy takes a good look at the store front and walks in.

He spots a bunch of hats in the back and walks over there. Looking through the hats he finds nothing of what he is looking for. A sales lady walks up to him and asks, "can I help you?" Randy looks at her and answers, "yeah, I'm look for 2 souvenir hats like the ones the guards at Buckingham Palace ware." She smiles and says, "that is a popular item, unfortunately we sold the last one last night." Randy thanks her and walks out.

Randy looks at the sheet of paper and realizes the next store is just 8 blocks away. A bus happens to be approaching that is going his way. Randy gets on, pays his fare, and sits down. He thinks to himself, "I hope the next one does." The driver calls out street names as they drive by. When Randy hears the name of the street he is looking for he pulls the stop cord and gets off at his stop.

He walks in the next store. It looks like a ghost town on the inside. Randy takes a look around, but doesn't find anything. He can't even find the store clerk. He shouts, "hello!" Finally, an older man walks in and asks, "can I help you?" Randy explains what he is looking for, and the clerk tells him they quit selling them last month. Randy thanks the clerk and walks out the store.

He checks his list and realizes the 3rd store is at least 2 miles away. He spots a taxi cab parked about a half a block away. He walks up to it and sees the driver sitting in the car reading the newspaper. He gets in and tells the driver where he wants to go. The driver puts down his newspaper and takes off.

The driver gets the car moving at 50 m.p.h. on a road where the speed limit is 40. Passing up cars left and right. Randy yells, "slow down!", but the driver keeps driving like a raving maniac. He even takes corners too fast, runs through a red light, and Randy feels like he's going to have a heart attack. The driver pulls up to the address that Randy gave him and says, "here you are." Randy pays him and gets out.

Randy thinks to himself, "someone ought to report him." The driver then takes off and drives like an old lady. Randy notices that the store he wanted has gone out of business. He sits down on a nearby bench and rests.

After about 10 minutes of resting, he takes a look at the sheet of paper he has for the last store on his list. He thinks to himself, "if they don't have it then I'm out of luck." He realizes that the store he needs is just 3 blocks away. He gets up and starts walking towards it.

On his way to the store, Randy notices 2 police cars with flashing light on parked outside an apartment building. He also notices a small crowd of on lookers. He feels it best to stay and watch with the on lookers. "What's going on?" asks Randy. A young man answers him, "they arrested the axe killer." Randy says quietly, "oh really." The young man then says, "yeah, they found him at his 3rd floor apartment sunbathing on the balcony."

A few minutes later, 2 police officers walk out of the apartment building with a shirtless 14-year-old boy in handcuffs. The boy yells, "I tell you, I didn't do anything, I was framed." One of the cops says to him, "yeah sure, tell it to the judge, just remember, we found a blood stained axe in your bedroom." The cops then put the boy in the squad car, accidently bumping his head on the roof.

The Police chief walks out shortly after that, carrying in his left hand an axe with the tag, "exhibit A" written on it. Then in his right hand he is carrying the boy's shirt. The cops get in their cars and take off sounding their sirens. Randy looks up at a 3rd floor window and sees the boy's parent in tears, as they can't believe that their son committed such a crime.

The crowd starts to break up and Randy resumes walking to the store. When he arrives at the store he sees what he is looking for in the display window. He puts on a big smile and goes in.

The store manager notices Randy right away. He walks up to Randy and says, "can I help you?" Randy smiles and says, "yes I'd like 2 hats just like the ones you got in your display window." The manager directs Randy to a table in the back of the room and tells him to check those out.

Randy walks over to the table and starts looking at the hats. After about 5 minutes he finds 2 hats in the sizes that would fit Mark and Scott. He takes both of them and walks over to the check-out counter. The manager then asks, "would you like me to wrap those in boxes for you?" Randy thinks for a second and replies, "yes, that would be great."

The manager wraps up the hats and then rings them up on the register. Randy pays for them and says, "my boys are just going to love these." The manager looks at Randy and asks, "how many kids do you have?" Randy answers, "just 2, Mark age 10 and Scott age 8." The manager smiles and says, "I hope your boys love those hats. Randy thanks him and leaves the store.

Thinking about the rough taxi ride he just got, Randy decides to take the bus back. He recalled seeing a bus going his way while watching the axe killer getting arrested. He walked back that way and found a small bus shelter. Looked at the bus schedule and saw that a bus was coming in 10 minutes.

When the bus shows up, he gets on and pays his fare. He sits down next to a lady holding 2 grocery bags. The lady notices the boxes and asks if they are for his wife or kids. He tells her about his kids at home, she smiles and gets off at the next stop. Randy thinks what a nice lady.

Randy gets off at his stop and starts walking toward his hotel. He gets to thinking he should try calling that cop again. He walks into his room and places the boxes on a table and sits down. He dials the number and this time the cop answers. Randy then says, "this is Captain Randy Miller calling you back, I understand you have some questions a dog that was kidnapped."

The cop then tells him, "we were wondering if you seen or heard anything that could give us a clue as to who may have done this?" Randy is quiet for a few seconds then says, "I heard a dog bark 3 times at 4:30 in the morning the day Buster disappeared. It sounded like Buster, I got up and looked out the window, but saw nothing." The cop thanked Randy for the information and they both got off the phone.

Randy starts thinking about the fact that he is returning home tomorrow. Now he could picture in his mind how excited Mark and Scott will be when he gets home with those guard hats. He also gets to thinking about how Buster has been missing for a while now and it looks doubtful that they will find him.

CHAPTER

4

Mark and Scott wake up a couple of days after Buster's disappearance. They get out of bed and walk downstairs wearing only their pajama bottoms. They see their mother sitting in a chair in the living room reading the newspaper. They both say good morning to her. She puts down her newspaper for a while and says, "good morning boys." Then puts her paper back up.

The boys walk into the kitchen, then Mark asks, "what's for breakfast?" Elaine then answers, "you boys can fix yourselves a bowl of cereal and toast today." The boys grab some cereal and milk and start making breakfast. Elaine then calls out to her boy's, "after you boys get dressed, you can go over to the Hanson's house. We're all going over to make posters of Buster and put them up all over town."

Mark and Scott start eating their cereal then Scott asks, "does dad come home today?" Elaine answers, "I think he gets home late tonight." Mark looks at his brother and says, "Do you think dad will have any interesting stories to tell us about London?" Scott looks right back at him and says, "you know he probably will." The boys finish their cereal and start making toast.

While the boys are making their toast, Mark asks his mom, "hey mom, what are we doing for the 4th of July weekend?" Elaine answers, "we along with the Hanson's are going to the cabin in Lake Geneva,

WI." Mark and Scott look excited. Then Mark replies, "that should be fun." The boys get done making their toast and sit down at the table.

Elaine puts her newspaper down and says, "I'm going over to the Hanson's now. I'll see you boys when you get there." She gets up and walks out.

Mark and Scott finish eating and then Mark says, "we beter get ready." Scott looks at his brother and asks, "wouldn't it be weird if we found Buster on the way there?" Mark smiles and answers, "it would be, but I doubt it." The boys put their dishes away, and head upstairs.

After the boys get dressed they leave the house and start walking towards the Hanson's house. Just before they get there, Kyle Smith meet up with them. "What are you losers up to now?", asks Kyle. Mark gets a little mad and replies, "go away!" Kyle starts to talk like a bully, "oo, I'm so scared." Mark yells, "will you please just go away?!" Kyle starts to walk away and says, "fine, I'll beat you up later."

Mark and Scott walk up to the front door and ring the doorbell. Josh answers the door and says, "come in, Tyler and I have been waiting for you." They walk in and sit down on the couch in the living room. Joyce and Elaine are sitting at the kitchen table looking at pictures of Buster.

Joyce calls out to the boys, "you boys come over here, we need help selecting a picture of Buster for the posters we're going to put up." The boys sit at the table and start looking at pictures. After a couple minutes, Scott finds a picture of Buster sitting in front of his doghouse. "How about this one?", asks Scott. Joyce looks at the picture and says, "that's perfect."

Joyce takes the picture from Scott and holds it up in front of her. Then she says, "wat do you think guys?" Everyone looks at the picture and all agree that it is the best picture to use of Buster. Joyce smiles and says, "good, now let's start designing posters."

Everyone grabs a sheet of paper and some markers. "Don't forget, David said to put reward $500 on the posters and put mine and David's cell phone number.", said Joyce. Everyone gets busy coloring posters. After about 10 minutes, everyone has at least 1 poster made.

Joyce then takes all the posters and puts them together side by side. After thinking it over, Joyce says, "I can't decide, let's take a vote. Every point to the one you like best." Most everyone votes for the one that Tyler made. Joyce grabs the poster Tyler made and tapes the picture of

Buster on it. She then takes it and says, "I'm going to go make some copies and be right back. Wait here for me." She then walks out the door.

Josh, Tyler, Mark, and Scott run upstairs to Josh's bed room while Elaine sits in the living room to keep an eye on Kimberly. Up in Josh's bedroom, the boys start thinking of a game they can play. Josh goes through some board games that he has. "How about clue?", asks Josh. Mark says, "that would be fine." While the other boys just nod their heads and say, "yeah, that's o.k."

Josh starts setting up and Mark says, "I want to be Colonel Mustard. Josh looks strait at Mark and says, "no way, I'm Colonel Mustard." Scott and Tyler look at each other and start chanting, "Fight! Fight! Fight!" Mark looks at Tyler and Scott; then tells them they aren't going to fight. Tyler and Scott look disappointed and together say, "darn!"

Josh sits quiet for a few seconds then says, "how are we going to settle this?" Scott suggests flipping a coin, but then Mark insists on a contest of skill or something.

After a few minutes Mark comes up with an idea and says, "how about we arm wrestle for it?" Josh laughs and says, "I'll beat you to easy." Mark looks strait at Josh and says, "I'll bet you 50 cents that I'll win." Josh laughs and says, "you're on." Mark and Josh make their bet and get ready to arm wrestle.

As soon as Mark and Josh get their arms up, Tyler grabs a hold of both hands and says, "get ready, set, wrestle!" Mark and Josh start arm wrestling, with their arms slowly moving back and forth. Their faces start to turn red as both boys put in all their effort. Scott starts cheering for Mark, and Tyler starts cheering for Josh. Mark's arm starts to tire, and Josh wins. Marks sticks his right hand down his pocket and pulls out 2 quarters and hands them to Josh and says, "you win, here you go."

The boys continue setting up the game with Josh being Colonel Mustard. After 15 minutes of playing, Joyce returns home. Tyler then says, "it sounds like mom's home." Scott sits up and says, "lets cheat and find out who did it." The other boys agree and Scott pulls out the cards and says, "it was Mr. Green, in the study, with the candlestick."

The boys put away the game and run downstairs. Joyce then says, "is everyone ready to put up posters?" Elaine then looks up, with Kimberly sitting in her lap and says, "we're ready." Joyce smiles and says, "I'll grab a couple of staple guns and we'll go." Joyce runs off and returns with

2 staple guns. Then Joyce says, "everybody in the car, Elaine can ride in the front with me, you kids in the back. Josh I need you to buckle Kimberly in her car seat between you and Tyler."

Once everyone is in the car, Joyce starts to back the car out of the garage. Scott whispers into Tyler's ear, "watch this." Then speaks a little louder, "are we there yet?" Elaine looks back at Scott and says, "you're a regular comedian." The boys all laugh.

A few minutes later they all arrive in the business district of Deerfield. Joyce parks the car and they all get out and meet on the sidewalk. Joyce hands out 10 posters and a staple gun to Josh and says, "you boys go across the street and put up posters on every telephone pole and wherever else you can and meet us back here when you're done."

The boys walk across the street and start putting up posters. They walk by an ice cream parlor and see through the window, some girls they know from school. They decide to walk in and say hello. The boys walk up to the table where they find the girls sitting their mother.

Mark makes a slight smile and says, "hello Katie, Jessica, and Mrs. Benson." Jessica blushes a little bit because she has a crush on Tyler and he doesn't know it. Mrs. Benson looks at Mark and says, "would you boys like to join us for some ice cream?" Mark looks at Mrs. Benson and says, "no thank you, we just stopped in to say hi to the girls, then continue putting up these posters." Then Tyler asks, "where's Ryan?" Mrs. Benson replies, "he's at baseball practice, we're going to do some shopping and pick him up later."

The boys say goodbye to Mrs. Benson and the girls and resume putting up posters. On the way out, Josh notices a bulletin board and decides to take some of the thumb tacks and put a poster on it.

Next the boys come across their favorite hobby shop. Figuring they all know the owner pretty well, they decide to ask him if they could borrow some tape and put up some posters on the store window. When the owner sees the boys to come over to his counter. When they get there he says, "look at this new model race car that just came in today." The boys look at it and are greatly impressed.

Josh then says, "that's a cool car." The owner then tells them he can sell it to them for $19.95. The boys talk quietly to themselves about what a great deal that is. Scott then says to the owner, "I have a birthday in August, maybe I could get it then." Then the owner says, "that would be fine." Josh then asks if they could tape a poser on the store window. The owner tells them to go ahead, they tape it up and leave.

Meanwhile on the other side of the street, Elaine, Joyce, and Kimberly are getting all their posters up. "I wonder how well the boys are doing?", asks Elaine. Joyce replies, "they seem to be doing well, I looked about a minute ago and they have a bunch up." They spot a laundromat and go in.

Once in, Elaine takes a poster and thumb tacks it up on the bulletin board in the back. Joyce notices a black lady in the laundromat having trouble with the change machine. She hits and yells at it, but the machine won't take here dollar. Joyce gets out a crisp dollar and exchanges it for the black lady's wrinkled dollar. The lady thanks her for her help and then they leave.

Joyce then says, "we're out of posters, let's go back to the car and wait for the boys." When they get back to the car they find the boys waiting there. They all get in and leave.

When they all arrive back at the Hanson's house they get out of the car and Joyce says, "Elaine and I are going to have some tea and coffee cake. Would you boys like to join us?" The boys stand in a huddle and talk quietly. Then Josh breaks away from the huddle and says, "no thanks mom, we decided that we want to hang out at Mark and Scott's tree house." Joyce then replies, "o.k. you boys go and have fun, but be home in a couple hours." Josh then answers, "o.k. mom we'll see you." Then the boys walk of.

Elaine, Joyce, and Kimberly walk in the house. Elaine sits down at the kitchen table and Kimberly takes her spot at the table with the booster seat. Joyce then asks, "Kimberly, would you prefer cookies and apple juice?" Kimberly looks up and quietly says, "yes." Joyce starts making tea, then pours apple juice in a small cup and puts a sippy lid on it, she then hands Kimberly the cup and 3 cookies.

Joyce then sits down at the table and says, "the tea will be ready shortly." Elaine looks at Kimberly for a moment and says, "Kimberly sure is growing up fast." Joyce smiles and says, "yes, David and I have been talking about putting her in preschool. We haven't made a decision yet." Elaine thinks for a moment then replies, "don't wait too long, I hear registration is going quickly." Just then the tea kettle whistles and Joyce gets up and pours the tea and serves up the coffee cake.

Back at the Miller's house, the boys climb into the tree house. Mark then says, "wouldn't be cool if someone found Buster and called your mom and dad today?" Josh looks at Mark and says, "yes that would be cool." Scott gets a little excited and says, "hey, maybe someone is calling your mom now." Josh rolls his eyes and explains, "that would be great, but most likely wishful thinking."

Kyle Smith then walks in the back yard looking for everyone. He yells, "hey guys, where are you?" Mark spots Kyle and talks in a soft voice, "everybody duck, we don't want Kyle to find us." The boys duck down and keep quiet. Kyle looks around and yells, "I know that you're back here, I saw you walk back this way." He looks up at the tree house and thinks, "I bet they're up there." He starts to climb up.

Mark sits up and says, "go away Kyle, we don't want you in our tree house club." Kyle steps down and says, "ah why not?" Mark looks a little frustrated and says, "if you hadn't been busy bullying everyone the last couple of years we would consider it." Kyle looks down at the ground then back up and says, "I promise not to beat you guys up anymore." Mark yells, "there's something fishy about that. Let me think about it for a few days." Kyle then walks away.

Back at Hanson's Joyce and Elaine are enjoying their tea. Elaine takes a sip of tea and says, "great tea." Joyce's cell phone rings and she answers, "Hello? Can you describe him? No, I'm sorry, Buster is a little taller. Thanks for calling." Joyce hangs up and eats a little coffee cake. Elaine sips her tea and says, "I thought for sure someone found Buster."

Kimberly accidently drops a cookie on the floor near Elaine. Elaine picks it up and hands it to Joyce to put it in the garbage. Joyce looks at Elaine and says, "we must think positively, someone will call on a lead to Buster's where about." Elaine nods her head yes and says, "yeah I'm sure we'll find him." Joyce sips her tea and says, "I hope so, the police don't have any real clues to go on."

A fly starts buzzing around the kitchen table. Joyce and Elaine watch it to see where it lands. After about a minute, the fly lands in the center of the table, Joyce swats it and says, "good, got rid of that pest."

Joyce's cell phone rings and she answers, "hello? Yes, I did put up a poster about a missing dog. No our dog is a German Shepherd. Thanks for calling.", She hangs up. Elaine looks at Joyce and says, "that was so close." Joyce speaks quietly, "I thought so too." Elaine thinks for a moment and says, someone will call in with Buster, just wait."

Back at the tree house the boys are laughing at the way they got rid of Kyle. The boys high five and then Mark says, "now we can have fun." Just then, Katie and Jessica Benson walk in the back yard. Katie looks up at the tree house and says, "hi boys!" The boys all look down and Mark asks, "what do you want?" Katie replies, "can we come up and play?" Mark looks a little angry and answers, "no girls aloud." The girls look shocked then Katie says, "but you told Kyle to go away." Mark starts to get frustrated and says, "it's different for him, he's a bully."

The girls finally had enough and leave. The boys high five as the girls leave and Scott says, "good, now we can have some fun." Josh then smiles and says, "so what do you guys want to do?" Things are silent in the tree house for a moment and then Tyler says, "let's play go to the dump." The boys all agree and Mark gets out the cards and starts to deal.

CHAPTER

The next day Randy wakes up at 10:00 a.m. after his long flight back from London. He gets dressed and has breakfast. While eating he looks out the window and sees Mark and Scott playing in the tree house. He asks his wife if anything interesting happened while he was away. She tells him about putting up posters of Buster all over town and having tea with Joyce.

Randy finishes eating breakfast then he grabs the 2 guard hats that he brought back from London. He walks out to the backyard and over to the tree house. He yells for the boys and both boys yell, "dad!" Then Randy says, "will you two get down here?" Both boys climb down as fast as they can, then they stop and stand in front of Randy.

Randy then says, "here are those guard hats I promised." The boys take the hats and Mark says, "wow! They're great!" Scott then says, "yeah dad, they're awesome." Both boys hug Randy. After a few seconds of hugging Randy, their dad says, "well why don't you put them on?" Mark and Scott put on the hats and Randy says, "they look great on you guys."

The boys decide they want to pretend they really are Buckingham palace guards, so they run to the center of the front yard and stood still just like the real guards. Randy then returns to the house. Once in he tells Elaine how the boys love their hats. They take a look out the front window and see the boys standing there. Then Randy says, "you know they'll get tired of this fast."

The 2 boys just stand there, as cars drive by the drivers slow down to look at them. Some give them a weird look, and others just scratch their heads. Everyone thinks, "how strange."

Kyle notices the boys standing there, so he walks up to them. "What are you guys doing?", he asks. The boys say nothing. Then he asks, "are you guys pretending to be palace guards?" Still they say nothing. Then Kyle says, "well, if you are, then there's nothing to prevent me from punching you." Then he takes his right hand and makes a fist and moves to punch Mark. Kyle then puts up his left hand and stops the punch 2 inches from Mark's face. Mark doesn't even flinch.

Kyle gets bored with pestering Mark and leaves. Mark and Scott stand outside like palace guards for a few more minutes. Then Mark says, "this is boring." Scott looks at his brother and says, "I was hoping you'd say that." The boys take off their hats and Mark says, "I wonder how the real guards do this without going nuts." Scott nods his head and says, "yeah." Then the boys walk in the house.

Once in they put their hats in their bedroom. Then they walk into the living room and they find Randy sitting on the couch reading the newspaper. "hey dad, did anything interesting happen to you in London?" Randy puts down his newspaper and says, "as a matter of fact, yes. I have a couple of stories to tell you."

"I read in a local newspaper a news story about a 14-year-old boy that murdered 3 people with an axe." Mark and Scott have a discussed look on their face and Mark says, "how disgusting." Then Randy continues, "well as it turns out, I got to witness the kid that did this get arrested right in front of me." Mark takes a short moment to think and says, "I wonder why someone would do such a thing."

Randy then replies, "I'm not sure, but as if that wasn't enough, I also had to deal with a raving manic cab driver." Mark and Scott look very interested and Randy continues, "first he drives like Uncle Fred on his way home, then after I got out of the car, he drove like Grandma Martha."

The boys thank their father for such great stories then ran up to their bedroom and put their hats away. They decided to go back out to their tree house. Once back up, Scott asks his brother, "so now what do you want to do?" Mark shrugs his shoulders and says, "I don't know." Scott thinks for a second and says, "we can play I spy."

Mark says, "I spy with my little eye something green." Scott looks around and says, that's easy, the grass." Mark laughs and says, "nope." Scott looks around and says, "The patio chairs." Mark smiles and says, "right." Just then Josh and Tyler walk in and look up at the tree house.

Josh then says, "hey guys can we come up?" Mark yells down to them, "what's the password?" Josh and Tyler stick their hands up their shirts and place them under their armpits and make 2 armpit farting noises. Mark then tells them to come up.

Scott then asks Josh if anyone found Buster yet, but Josh reports nothing new. Scott mentions that they were playing I spy, then Josh says, "how lame." Then Mark says, "do you have any better ideas?" Josh answers, "not really." Scott asks, "can we go swimming at your house?" Josh replies, "no, mom and dad are cleaning out the pool." All the boys look clueless for a while then Mark says, "lets spy on Mrs. Jones next door, she often doing something funny."

The boys crawl down low to the back window and pop their heads just above the lower portion of the window. They can see Mrs. Jones mopping the kitchen floor and dancing to some music. The boys all laugh because it looks so funny to them. Mrs. Jones then walks into the living room for a while. The boys move away from the window.

Josh then says, "any more bright ideas?" Scott replies, let's just go play some basketball at your house." The boys all agree and climb down to go to the Hanson's house.

Once there, Josh gets out the basketball and they decide to play Josh and Tyler against Mark and Scott. They tip off the ball and Tyler gets the ball first. Scott goes to guard Tyler and Mark guards Josh. Tyler spots Josh with a slight opening and passes the ball to Josh. Josh shoots and scores. The game goes on for more than 10 minutes and the Millers win by a score of 10-7.

After the game the boys decide to rest, so they go to the backyard and sit down at the picnic table. Mark looking across the back end of the backyard towards Buster's doghouse, and says, "I wonder if the cops overlooked something when they investigated Buster's kidnapping." Josh looks at Mark and says, "I guess they could have."

Tyler then says, "maybe we can do some investigating ourselves." Scott gets excited and says, "we could call ourselves the junior crime detectives." Then Tyler gets excited and says, "junior crime detectives! Wait right here." Tyler gets up and runs into the house. The other boys puzzled as to what he is doing now.

Tyler runs up to his bedroom and opens up a closet, and starts going through a bunch of boxes starts saying to himself, "where is it? Where is it? Where is it?", Then a final shout, "WHERE IS IT?!!!!!!!!!!", Then he comes across a box labeled junior crime detective kit. He opens up the box and takes out the contents.

Inside the box he finds a Sherlock Holms cap, a cape, a magnifying glass, and a plastic toy pipe that blows bubbles. He pours some soap solution in the pipe, grabs the other things and goes outside.

Once outside, he puts on the cap and cape and returns to the picnic table. Josh takes one look at him and asks, "Ah Tyler, why did you go and get something like that?" Tyler blows some bubbles with his pipe and answers, "If we're going to be junior crime detectives, I think at least one of us should look the part." Scott takes a look at him and says, "I think he looks cool. Where did you get that?" Tyler smiles and says, "Aunt Jenny gave it to me last Christmas."

Josh then rolls his eyes then whispers to himself, "my goofy brother." Mark then says, "so what are we going to do next?" Josh thinks for a moment and replies, "wait a minute, I'll get a flashlight and we can take a closer look at Buster's doghouse." Josh gets up and leaves.

Josh returns with a flashlight and says, "come on, let's go over to Buster's doghouse." The boys get up and start walking. David notices the boys walking over to the doghouse and yells, "hey Josh, where are you going?" Josh then answers we're going look and see if there is a clue that the police didn't see." David then thinks to himself, "ha, ha, ha. Those boys and their silly games." Then he says, "have fun." Josh looks at David and says, "we will dad."

When they get to the doghouse, Josh tells Tyler to look outside the doghouse with his magnifying glass while he looks inside with a flashlight. "What are we looking for?", asks Tyler. "Anything, blood, finger prints, anything that the kidnapper left behind.", answers Josh. Mark and Scott move in and get a closer look.

Tyler begins to look with his magnifying glass and only sees chipped paint. Josh is looking inside with a flashlight. "Does anyone see anything?", asks Josh. "Only chipped paint.", answers Scott. Josh looks around some more and says, "keep looking."

The boys take a closer look and finally Josh says, "ah ha! The kidnapper wasn't as careful as the cops thought!" Josh crawls out of the doghouse, and continues talking, "he left behind this bubble gum wrapper." Tyler looks at Josh and says, "so he left behind a bubble gum wrapper, so what?" Josh then answers, "it's a Gregory gum wrapper, the kind of gum that only be bought at Wayne's drugstore in Northbrook."

Mark gets to thinking about Josh's find and says, "so let's get over to Wayne's drugstore and question Wayne." Scott replies, "that's about 5 miles away, mom and dad won't let us go that far on our bikes." The boys sit and think for a while. Mark comes up with an idea and says, "hey I know, I remember my dad taking the bus to the airport a couple weeks ago when his car was in the shop. I can run home and get the schedule." Josh then says, "what are you waiting for, go get it." Mark runs off.

When Mark returns with the schedule, he opens it up and looks for the next time a bus leaves town for the airport. After about a minute he says, "according to this, the next bus starts to leave town in about 20 minutes from now, and we can catch it 2 blocks from that park we play at." Josh replies, "that's fantastic, does everyone have enough bus fair?" The boys check their pockets and see that they do.

As the boys start to walk off, David yells to Josh, "Josh, your mother and I will have the pool ready in about an hour if you boys want to go swimming later." Josh answers, "o.k. thanks dad." The boys wave goodbye to Joyce and David as they head off. On their way they come across Katie and Jessica Benson. "What are you boys up to?", asks Katie. Tyler answers, "we're investigating a crime." Jessica notices the outfit Tyler is wearing and says, "I love a man in uniform." Then she kisses him on the right cheek. Tyler takes the back of his right hand and wipes his right cheek and says, "yuck!"

The boys continue walking to the bus stop. When they get there, Josh looks at his watch and says, "good, we now have about 8 minutes till the bus comes." The boys wait patiently for the bus. A short while goes by, and the boys are pacing like it's taking forever. Once they see it they get excited and ready to board.

They get on board the bus and pay their fare. They walk back 5 rows and Mark and Scott take seats on the left. Josh and Tyler take the seats on the right. They look around the bus and see there are only 2 other passengers. One is an old lady siting in the 2nd row seat on the left. She is busy talking to a friend on her cell phone. The other is a 30-year-old black guy sitting in the back row on the right half asleep. They look at each other and wonder why he is so sleepy.

As the bus moves on, they pick up other passengers, some look at Tyler and wonder why he is wearing that hat and cape. Josh tells his brother not to blow bubbles on the bus, it might bother some of the passengers. One man sitting behind Tyler asks him why is he wearing that outfit. Tyler explains, we're investigating a crime."

"What kind of crime?", asks the man. "Kidnapping.", answers Tyler. "Sounds like a serious crime.", says the man. Tyler looked back at him and said, "it is serious, someone kidnapped our dog." The man thinking, they are just playing a game sits back and says, "well I hope you find who did it." Tyler turns and faces the front of the bus.

The boys see a sign that says welcome to Northbrook and get excited. Then Josh reminds everyone that Wayne's drugstore is a little more than 1 mile away. However, they know they have to be watching for their stop. Josh then starts looking out the window for their stop.

The driver is calling out street names as they move on. The boys are listening for him to call their stop. Scott says, "we're almost there now." The bus comes to a stop just 2 blocks away from the store, 3 people get off and 2 get on. Tyler then says, "our stop is next." The bus gets moving again and Josh signals for a stop. When the bus gets to their stop, the boys get off and thank the driver for the ride.

Tyler starts to blow bubbles right after he gets off the bus. Josh then asks, "are you going to be blowing bubbles the whole time?" Tyler answers, "no just every now and then." As the boys approach the drugstore Josh says, "let's not go straight to Wayne. Let's pretend to be customers and look at the comic books first."

They casually walk to the magazine rack, pick up some comic books and pretend to read. Josh peaks over the top of his comic book and sees Wayne at the counter helping a customer then he looks back down. After Wayne is finished with his customer, he notices the boys at the magazine rack and walks over.

"Can I help you?", asks Wayne. The boys put down their comic books and put them away. "Well, I'm waiting.", says Wayne. Josh takes a deep breath and says, "well, it's like this, we we're wondering if you saw any suspicious looking people buying this gum within the last couple of weeks?" Josh hands Wayne the gum wrapper. Wayne takes the gum wrapper and asks, "what?"

Tyler takes the pipe out of his mouth, points the mouth piece at Wayne and says, "sir, don't you know it's a federal offence to withhold information from the authorities?" He puts the pipe back in his mouth and blows bubbles. Wayne then asks, "what are you kids doing? Playing some sort of game?"

Josh starts to look like he's losing his cool. Mark decides to take over and says, "look mister, we're junior crime detectives and we're looking for the guy who bought that gum." Wayne points to Tyler and says, "so that's why he is in such a goofy outfit." Scott looks at Wayne and asks, "can you help us out or not?"

"Well I'm sorry boys, but most of my customers that buy that gum are kids your age.", said Wayne. Josh looking a bit disappointed says, "you mean you saw no suspicious looking adults within the last 2 or 3 weeks buy that?" Wayne thinks for a moment and answers, "no one I can think of." Josh thanks Wayne for his help and asks if they can question other employees. Wayne agrees and the boys move on.

First they question a stock boy, but got no help. Next they talk to the lady working in the photo lab, but no help there. The cosmetics lady and the guy working in the pharmacy had no help as well. The boys give up and walk out. They walk across the street and sit on the bus bench waiting to catch the bus home.

Looking disappointed, Josh holds up the gum wrapper and says, "I can't believe nobody saw who bought this." Tyler looks at Josh and says, "hey let me look at that." Josh hands the wrapper to Tyler and he looks at it with his magnifying glass and says, "ah ha and ah ha!" The rest of the boys get excited thinking Tyler stumbled onto a new clue. "What is it?" asks Josh. Tyler replies, "I remember this gum wrapper, I was chewing this gum while playing with Buster in the backyard a few weeks ago. I must have dropped the wrapper on the ground and the wind blew it in the doghouse."

All the boys yell, "oh Tyler!", and they lightly hit Tyler on the back of his head. Just then the bus shows up and they get on.

On the way home one of Joyce Hanson's friends named Barbra recognizes Josh and Tyler. She gets to thinking that the boys are too young to ride the bus alone, so she calls Joyce on her cell phone. She explains everything to Joyce, and Joyce isn't pleased with what she hears because Josh is only 11 and Tyler is only 9. Joyce tells her she will talk to her boys and pass this information to Elaine.

The boys get off at the stop near the park and walk to the park. When they get there, they find Kyle on the seesaw with a friend. They see the 2 laughing which is something they never saw before. Mark says, "that's odd, he's normally beats guys up." The boys go over to the merry go round and get on.

Scott then asks, "so what do we do now, we're not junior crime detectives anymore?" Josh then replies, "let's just stay here for a while, maybe we'll think of something." Mark then says, "too bad that wrapper didn't turn up something, we could have been heroes."

Kyle and his friend get of the seesaw and walk over to merry go round. Mark then says, "don't look now but here comes trouble." Kyle stops the merry go round and says, "I know you guys hate me, and I've given you plenty of reason to hate me, but I want to change that." Mark looks at Kyle and says, "what do you really want?" There is a short moment of silence then Kyle answers, "I want to be a member of your tree house club."

Mark takes a deep breath and replies, "that whole idea sounds fishy to me, but I'll tell you what, we're going to the cabin for the 4th of July. When we get back, we'll put you through the club house initiation." Kyle thanks Mark and he, along with his friend leave.

Josh asks Mark, "are you really going to let Kyle in the club house?" Mark spits on the ground and replies, "if I play my cards right, he won't want to join." All the boys smile. Tyler then says, "come on, let's go home, maybe we can go swimming now." Josh looks at Tyler and says, "yeah and you can get out of that goofy outfit." The boys get off the merry go round and walk home.

On the way home the boy come across Katie and Jessica. Tyler tries to hide from Jessica, but it doesn't work. Jessica runs up to him and says, "my conquering hero." Then she kisses him on the right cheek. Tyler wipes his right cheek with the back of his right hand and says, "yuck!" Josh replies, "some hero, we got nowhere trying to solve the case." Jessica smiles and says, "well at least you tried."

Katie then looks at Josh and says, "we're going to go roller skating, do you boys want to join us?" Josh shacks his head no and says, "not this time." The girls walk off and Mark says, "ha! Ha! Tyler's got a girlfriend!" Tyler gets a little angry and says, "she's not my girlfriend,

I'm too young to have a girlfriend." Josh laughs and replies, "so why does she love you?" Tyler answers, "I used to sit next to her in school, and I sat with her during lunch 1 time."

Josh, Mark, and Scott all start to tease Tyler saying, "Tyler and Jessica sitting in a tree, k-i-s-s-i-n-g." Tyler interrupts, "shut up! Shut up! Shut up! SHUT UP!" The other boys stop, then Josh says, "o.k. we'll stop." The boys decide they want to go swimming, so Mark and Scott continue walking to their house and Josh and Tyler go into their house.

Once in Joyce tells them her friend Barbra called and told her about the bus ride. Josh and Tyler were told they were grounded. Elaine told Mark and Scott the same thing. The boys couldn't see their friends for a couple of days.

CHAPTER

6

I t was a rainy Thursday Morning in Aurora, IL. At about 8:17 a.m. there was a flash of lightning. 5 seconds later, thunder sounded that woke up Dan Fredrickson. His wife Shirley woke up a few seconds later. She looked at her husband and said, "dear, I want you to go out today and walk Buster." Dan replies, "I will if it stops raining."

"I just love how you got him for me as a 30th wedding anniversary present.", said Shirley. Some loud thunder sounds and Dan says, "I remember you telling me how much you loved having a German Shepherd when you were a little girl." Shirley kisses her husband and says, "thanks dear."

Dan gets out bed first. He takes his shower, gets dressed, and then eats breakfast. He then opens the front door to get the newspaper. Shirley then walks downstairs after she showers and gets dressed. Dan then goes into the living room and starts reading the newspaper. "Anything interesting in the news?", asks Shirley. "nothing so far", answered Dan.

Shirley turns on the kitchen radio then sits back down to finish eating breakfast. "I'm going to the store to get some dog treats for Buster. Would you like anything?", asked Shirley. Dan lowers his paper and says, "I know we need more bread." Just then the radio announcer comes on and announces the weather forecast. "The rain will be ending around mid-morning", he says.

Shirley looks at her husband and says, "did you hear that Dan? You should be able to walk Buster before lunch." Dan lowers his paper a little and says, "I guess I can."

Shirley finishes breakfast, grabs her purse, and says, "I'm off to the store, see you soon." Dan says goodbye to her and she walks out the door. She then gets in her car and drives off. While in the car she turns on the radio. As she is driving down the road she hears a soft jazz song that she likes and sings along with the music. When the song is over the news comes on.

She pulls into the parking lot of the store and gets out of the car. She looks up at the sky and thinks the rain should end shortly. Shirley walks in and picks up a basket. While looking at dog treats for buster, she bumps into her friend Beverley. "Oh hi Shirley, how are you doing?", asked Beverley. Shirley Looks over to her left and sees Beverley.

"I'm fine, how about you?", asked Shirley. "Just fine.", said Beverley. Shirley begins to put dog treats in her basket. She then finds a toy squeaker and puts it in her basket. Then Beverley asks, "how's that new dog Dan got you?" Shirley smiles and answers, "oh he's great, you should come over and see Buster, we just love him." Beverley tells Shirley that she will call her later and walks off.

Shirley walks over to the bread isle. Walks down a short distance and looks at some bread. She finds a big loaf of white bread and puts it in her basket. Then she makes her way to the check-out line and is standing behind a lady with a cart load of about 15 things. While in line, she spots a magazine for dog lovers. She picks it up and glances through it.

When the lady is finished, Shirley puts away the magazine. The cashier scans all of her items and tells her the total. Shirley swipes her bank card and signs for everything. She walks out the store and notices that the rain is dying down.

She gets into her car and starts off for home. She turns on the car radio and starts to sing along with the music. She really smiles when her favorite song comes on. She pulls up to a stoplight and stops. People walking by on the sidewalk see her singing and laugh because it looks so funny. She's so much into her music, she doesn't care. The light turns green and she continues home.

When she gets home, she greets Dan and walks to where Buster is sitting. She pulls out the toy squeaker and gives it to Buster. "Look at what I got Buster.", said Shirley. Dan looks up and says, "that's nice." Buster barks a couple of times, then Shirley says, "it looks like the sun may come out later." Buster gets into playing with his toy.

At 10:30 a.m. Dan decides to tack Buster for a walk. He grabs a leash and puts it on Buster. He tells his wife that he and Buster are going out. When he gets out he notices that the sky is clearing up and the sun may start shining. Dan then says, "come on Buster, let's go to the park."

On the way there, he walks by his neighbor's house. Fred just happens to be putting mail in his mailbox as Dan walks by. "Hello Dan.", said Fred. Dan looks over to Fred and stops by the mailbox and says, "oh hello Fred." Dan orders Buster to sit and Fred bends over and pets Buster on the head a couple of times. Fred then says, "so this must be that dog you told me that you bought for Shirley." Dan smiles and says, "ah you bet."

Fred pets Buster on the head 2 more times and says, "well, I'll let you continue on your walk." Fred walks in his house and Dan and Buster continue walking. Dan sees the park just up a head and tells Buster we're almost there.

Dan and Buster arrive at the park and walk on a trail for a third of a mile. Dan then finds a park bench and sits down and Buster sits beside him. He sees several kids playing on the playground equipment in front of him. 2 kids, a boy and a girl notice Dan and Buster. They decide to walk up and talk to Dan.

The boy talks to Dan first, "hey mister, what's your dog's name?" Dan looks at the boy and says, "his name is Buster." The girl then asks, "do you mind if we pet him?" Dan nods his head and answers, "sure, he loves to be petted, especially on the head." The kids start petting Buster. Dan then says, "would you look at that? It looks like he's enjoying it." The kids start laughing.

The mother of the 2 kids approaches and says, "Brendan! Sally! Get over here!" She points to the ground. Brendan then says to Dan, "sorry sir, we have to leave." The kids then get up and leave. When they get close to their mother, she says, "what did I tell you about talking to strangers? Now come on, we're going home." The mother and kids walk off.

Dan sits for a few more minutes and then his friend Mike walks up and says, "I thought that was you Dan." Mike sits on the bench next to Dan. Mike and Dan shake hands and Dan says, "well Mike, it's been a while since I've seen you." Mike thinks for a moment and says, "yeah, I think it's been a few months."

Mike looks at Buster and says, "when did you get him?" Mike points to Buster. Then Dan answers, "less than 2 weeks ago, on our 30th wedding anniversary." Mike looks impressed and says, "wow, your wife must be happy." Dan smiles and says, "she is." Mike gets up and says, "well I better get going, my wife is waiting at home for me." Mike then walks off.

Dan gets up and starts walking home. Shelley Conner, a friend of Joyce Hanson's spots Buster from the other end of the park. She thinks to herself, "that looks like Buster." She calls out to him, "here Buster!" She notices Buster looks toward her then Dan starts to walk at a faster pace. She decides to call Joyce.

Shelley starts searching through her purse looking for her cell phone. She finds her lipstick, then her wallet, but still nothing. Digs in deeper and finds 3 different types of combs, and pictures of her kids. She finally realized she left her phone at home. She starts walking only to be thinking about calling Joyce.

Dan realizing, he may have been spotted by someone who recognizes Buster decides to hurry home. He gets walking even faster and gets out of the park quickly. After leaving the park, he slows down a bit. He thinks to himself, "darn that lady on the other side of the park. I think she knows Buster, she called for him and he looked her way."

Dan returned home. He walked in the house looking tired. Shirley sees Dan walking in and sitting down on the couch. "Dan, you look tired", said Shirley, "what happened to you at the park?" Dan takes a couple of deep breathes and says, "Buster spotted a female dog and chased after her." Shirley takes Buster and tells Dan to rest up.

Shirley takes Buster in to the kitchen and gives him some dog treats. She thinks to herself, "wow, he must have had a lot of fun. I never seen Dan so tired after a walk before." Shirley picks up the newspaper and begins to read. After a few minutes of reading the news, she then turns to the variety page and reads an article on gardening tips.

When Shelley gets home, she finds her cell phone on the kitchen table. She sits down at the kitchen table, picks up her cell phone and dials Joyce's phone number. When Joyce answers, Shelley says, "Joyce you won't believe this, I was just at the park and I thought I saw Buster." Joyce sounds excited and Shelley continues, "I said here Buster! And the dog turned for a moment, like he recognized me."

Joyce asks if she for sure knew it was Buster, but Shelley said she couldn't be certain because he was way over on the other side of the park. Shelley went on to mention that the dog looked like Buster and the man that was walking him started to walk faster after she called for Buster. Joyce is now convinced that Shelley saw Buster. Shelley gets off the phone with Joyce and gets ready to go to church for choir practice.

At the Hanson house, Joyce calls for her boys to come downstairs. Josh and Tyler run down the steps and stop by where Joyce is standing. "I got some good news", said Joyce. The boys look surprised. Joyce continues, "you know my friend Shelley, who sings in the church choir?" Josh nods his head yes, but Tyler asks, "who's she?" Josh replies, "she sang oh come all ye faithful last Christmas Eve." Tyler then says, "oh yeah, I remember her."

"So what's the good news?", asks Josh. Joyce replies, "I just got a phone call from Shelley, she said she was at the park near her house, and she thought she saw Buster." The boys look excited. Joyce continues, "now don't get to excited, the dog she saw was a good distance away, there is a chance it wasn't Buster. Shelley just thought it was." Tyler then asks, "did she follow the guy walking that dog?" Joyce replies, "no, he got away before she could, now go wash up, I'm going to have lunch ready soon."

Dan and Shirley were just finishing lunch and Shirley says, "would you like to go to a movie this afternoon dear?" Dan sips his coffee and answers, "what's showing?" Shirley replies, "I'll check.", gets up and goes into the living room. She picks up the newspaper and sits on the couch and reads.

Dan looks at Shirley and says, "any good comedies showing?" Shirley looks things over and replies, "there's one starting in a half hour." Dan smiles and says, "great, let's go to it. I'll put Buster in his kennel and you get ready to go." Dan gets up and takes Buster outside to his kennel. Shirley grabs her purse and gets in the car. Dan locks up the kennel, and gets in the car with Shirley.

The 2 drive off together. They listen to news/talk radio on the way. They arrive 10 minutes early. They go in, buy their tickets, then get a large popcorn and 2 medium sodas. They walk in the theatre and find some good seats. They enjoy some quiet conversation as the previews start.

As the movie gets started they begin eating popcorn and drinking soda. They enjoy a few laughs and talk quietly about how they can relate to what they see. At one point in the movie some guy falls of the roof of his house while fixing some shingles, but the way he lands was very funny. Then the guy's wife comes out and yells at him.

After the movie Dan and Shirley walk out laughing and talking about the movie all the way to the car. They get in the car and talk about the great time they had. They get home and Shirley walks in the house and Dan goes and gets Buster. The whole time he's walking with Buster, he wonders how he would explain to his wife if Buster's real owners showed up looking for Buster. How would he explain having to kidnap Buster?

Dan walked in the house with Buster. He sees his wife talking on the phone with someone. Dan decides to go in the family room to watch some t.v. He finds a good baseball game and watches it. He finds out his favorite team is winning and is very pleased.

His wife gets off the phone and walks in the family room. She sits next to Dan and says, "I was just talking to Mike and Julie, they and the kids want to come over for dinner tonight. They can't wait to see Buster." Dan replies, "sure, that would be great, and I would love to see the grandchildren." Dan and Shirley look very excited as they watch the rest of the ball game together.

After the game, Shirley goes into the kitchen and starts on dinner. Just then the doorbell rings. Dan gets up and turns off the television and goes to answer the door. He opens the door and sees his son Mike and his wife Julie standing there with the kids. "Hello dad.", says Mike. Dan invites them in and they all sit down in the living room.

Dan smiles and says, "the kids are growing up fast, how old are they?" Mike replies, "Justin is 3 and Linda is 1." Just then Buster walks in the living room and sits near Dan. Then Mike says, "so that must be Buster, the dog mom told us about." Dan pets Buster a couple times and says, "yep, this is Buster."

The kids walk slowly towards Buster. Linda sits on the floor near Buster, but Justin starts to pet him. Julie notices Buster being friendly with the kids and says, "he sure gets along well with the kids." Dan replies, "yeah, he is very house broken." Dan, Mike, and Julie just sit there watching the kids petting Buster.

Shirley walks in the living room and announces that dinner is ready. Mike and Julie pick up the kids and they all go and sit down at the dinner table. Shirley puts the food on the table and they all start to dish up. Julie takes a jar of baby food and starts to feed Linda first. Mike encourages Justin to start eating, then they all begin to eat.

Shirley looks around the table then says, "so Julie, how's law school going for you?" Julie then replies, "I'm almost done, I'll be practicing law soon." Dan looks at her with interest like he may need her someday, but says nothing. Shirley then adds, "we'll have to celebrate when you're done." Julie smiles and says, "that would be great."

Mike looks at his wife and says, "she is looking forward to getting things done." Dan clears his throat and decides to change the conversation, so he says, "I hear you've been working hard Mike." After Mike finishes chewing on some food, he answers, "yeah I really have a lot of clients at the bank, handling their finances keeps me busy." Dan looks at Mike and says, "our neighbors told me what a great job you did helping them with their 401k." Mike smiles and says, "I do my best."

After dinner everyone gets up from the dinner table and goes out into the back yard. Dan grabs a tennis ball so they can play fetch with Buster. Once outside, Dan throws the tennis ball and yells, "fetch!" Buster runs and barks a couple times as he runs after the ball. When he gets it, he returns it to Dan. Mike then says, "come on dad, put some power in to it this time." Dan throws it hard and Buster returns and Mike gets it.

Mike gives it a good toss and Buster runs after it. Mike says, "he sure runs fast." Buster quickly returns with the ball and everyone has fun playing with Buster. After a half hour everyone goes back in.

Mike and Julie tell Dan and Shirley what a good time they had. They all hug and talk about getting together another time. They even suggest that Dan and Shirley stop over someday and bring Buster. Dan tells them they will and Mike and Julie go out the front door with the kids.

Late at night, Dan and Shirley are getting ready for bed. Shirley says, "that sure was a fun day with Mike and Julie. Dan looks at his wife and says, "it sure was, and seeing the grandchildren was great too." Dan kisses is wife just before she turns off the light and they get into bed. Once in bed and the lights are out, Dan thinks, "I hope Shirley never finds out that I kidnapped Buster."

CHAPTER

The Hansons are getting ready to go to Lake Geneva. David is busy loading suitcases in the car. Up in the boy's bedroom, Josh and Tyler fight over toys and games to take with. In the kitchen Kimberly is helping her mom load a cooler with some food. Joyce hears some noise upstairs. She takes Kimberly upstairs with her. When she gets there, she finds the boys fighting over a football.

"Boys!", she yells, "will you please stop fighting over that football?" The boys stop and Tyler says, "it's Josh's fault." Josh looks a little mad and says, "no, it's Tyler's fault." The boys fight some more and Joyce breaks it up. Joyce holds the 2 boys back and they keep trying to punch each other. Joyce says, "put that football away." She points to some toys and games on the floor. "You 2 are going to take Those 2 games and those 2 toys with you and that's it."

The boys stop fighting and resume getting ready for the trip. Joyce calmly says," I want you boys on your best behavior, we want Randy and Elaine Miller to continue inviting us to the lake." Josh looks right at his mom and says, "sorry mom, we will do beter", he looks at Tyler and continues, "right Tyler?" Tyler nods his head yes. Joyce and Kimberly return to the kitchen.

At the Miller's house, Mark and Scott are getting ready. While packing their suitcases Scott asks, "Should we bring any toys or games?" Mark answers, "no, we have plenty up there plus Josh and Tyler always bring stuff. Scott nods his head and says, "you're right." Elaine walks into the boy's room and asks, "are you boys almost ready?" Mark answers, "yes mom we are just about done." Elaine smiles and says, "good, your father is ready so bring your things down stairs."

Randy was busy loading the car with suitcases and then Mark and Scott walk out of the house with theirs. When they get to the car, Randy says, "thank you boys." Then he puts their suitcases in the trunk. Randy looks at his watch and says, "I wonder how your mother is doing with the cooler, she told me she would have it ready soon." Randy and the boys walk in the house.

Mark and Scott start whispering and giggling. "What's so funny boys?", asks Randy. Mark and Scott both answer at the same time, "nothing dad." Randy rolls his eyes and says, "you boys sure have a strange sense of humor. They walk into the kitchen and find Elaine packing a cooler.

"Do you have the cooler ready Elaine?", asks Randy. "I just got to add more ice and we're ready to go.", answers Elaine. She grabs a bag of ice out of the freezer and dumps the ice in. She then puts the lid on and shuts it tight. Randy grabs the cooler and caries it out to the car.

Elaine tells the boys to go to the bathroom one more time, so they won't have to stop on the way. She turns off the coffee maker and goes around the house turning off lights and getting ready to lock up and leave. The boys finish with the bathroom and they and Elaine go out the door and get in the car.

Randy starts the car and they head off. At the same time, the Hansons are leaving. Randy then says, "well guys, here we go on a weekend of fun." Elaine and the boys yell, "yay!" They get out onto open highway and start singing 99 bottles of beer on the wall. By the time they get down to 57 bottles Scott says, "this is boring, can we do something else?" They then are out in the country and see the cows in the farm fields, so they make up weird stories about the cows.

They drive past the welcome to Wisconsin sign. Then Mark says, "hey we just entered Wisconsin." Scott looks excited even though he knows they still have a long way to go. Mark points to a cow in the field and says, "well anyways, you see that cow over there?" Scott says, "yes." Mark continues, "he just burped, and that pond over there" points to a pond, "that's split pea soup for some giant." Everyone laughs and Elaine comments on what a sense of humor Mark has.

They arrive in Geneva and stop at the local store to pick up some things for the cabin. There is also a fireworks stand in the parking lot. Joyce and David arrive with their kids and Joyce, Elaine, and Kimberly go in the store to pick up groceries while David, Randy, and the boys go pick out fireworks for the 4th of July show at the lake.

Once they all get everything they need, they return to their cars and everyone gets in their own family's car, then they head off to the lake. They arrive at the lake cabin and David parks his car on the left side of the driveway and Randy on the Right. Everyone gets out and Randy says, "boys, you guys put the fireworks in the garage, in some high place where Kimberly can't get them and we will put the groceries away."

Randy unlocks the door on the side of the garage, then walks off with a bag of groceries. Each boy grabs a box full of fireworks and walk in the garage. They go to the back of the garage where there a work bench. Mark suggests putting the fireworks on the work bench. Each boy does what Mark said then goes out of the garage. Mark pushes the lock button on the door, then exits and checks to see if the door locked behind him. Josh points to the basketball hoop on the garage and asks about playing a game. Mark tells him later they can ask their parents to their cars so they can.

The boys walk in the cabin and find everyone still putting away groceries. Joyce and Elaine are trying to figure out where to put the watermelon. Mark says, "wow, that's one big watermelon." Meanwhile Kimberly is sitting on the floor of the living room watching cartoons on t.v. The boys decide to sit on the couch and watch with her.

After the food is put away they decide to have lunch. They start cooking some hotdogs and baked beans. Then Elaine opens a bag of potato chips. David and Randy sit down at the kitchen table and play some black jack. Elaine and Joyce set the table and announce lunch will be ready soon.

When Elaine announces that lunch is ready. David says, "o.k. you kids, get over to the table and eat." Mark turns off the television and the kids sit down at the table. Joyce sets up a booster chair and puts Kimberly in it. They say grace and start eating.

After lunch Josh asks, "hey mom, can us guys go swimming yet?" Joyce replies, "we have to put everything away and clean up first." David adds to that, "don't forget, our suitcases are still in the cars." Randy hands Mark his car keys and says, "why don't you and Scott go to our car and bring in our suitcases." David hands Josh his car keys and gives the same instructions to Josh and Tyler.

When the boys have finished bringing in all the suitcases, David says, "now you guys can go swimming." So the boys go into the boy's bedroom. After about 10 minutes, the boys come out wearing only their swimsuits and carrying their beach towels. When they get outside, they find Joyce and Elaine there and they take the time to spray on sun screen on all the boys. Once done with that, the boys run to the beach, put down their towels and jump off the dock.

Once in the lake the boys get into rough housing. The parents then walk down to the campfire area and sit down in lawn chairs. Kimberly then runs down and sits on Joyce's lap. The boys decide to have a chicken fight. So Scott gets up on Mark's shoulders and Tyler gets up on Josh's shoulders. Then the chicken fight begins. After a couple of minutes, Scott with a little help from Mark pulls Tyler off Josh's shoulders. Mark and Scott start to celebrate their victory.

Josh yells, "I want a rematch!" Mark and Scott agree to the rematch, so the boys set things up just like the first round. Round 2 gets started right away and ends shortly with Josh and Tyler as the winners. Josh and Tyler start celebrating when Mark demands a rematch. Josh then says, "sure, we'll do one more for a tie breaker, winner takes all."

Mark then asks, "what does the winner get after they win?" All the boys start thinking about it for a while. Then Josh says, "how about after we're done swimming, we go into the bedroom and the winners get to nipple twist the losers and hold that twist for one minute." Mark and Scott agree to the conditions and they shake hands with Josh and Tyler to make it an official bet.

The boys set everything up for round 3. Once they're ready they start the final chicken fight. After couple minutes, Josh and Tyler come up as winners. Mark and Scott each put their right hands on their chests and look down as they began to think about the pain they will feel when Josh and Tyler will get to twist their nipples later. They boys then resume their rough play in the lake for a while.

The boys finish swimming and get out the lake. They pick up their towels and dry off. Mark asks his dad why he didn't put on his swimsuit and jump in. Randy tells him, he's still groggy from flying round trip to Minneapolis yesterday then the drive to the lake today.

Mark knows his father will probably go swimming tomorrow. The boys walk into the house and go in their bedroom. The boys put their towels down on the floor and Josh says, "now to take care of some unfinished business." Mark sighs then says, "yes we know." Mark and Scott stand next to each other with their backs to the wall. Josh stands in front of Mark and Tyler in front of Scott. Josh and Tyler twist Mark and Scott's nipples and hold it for one minute.

When the nipple twisting is done, Josh and Tyler let go. Mark and Scott rub their chests for a moment and talk about how much that hurts. Josh and Tyler smile and Josh says, "it's supposed to hurt." Mark then replies, "yeah I know." The boys then get dressed and go out into the living room and watch some television.

Down at the campfire area the parents and Kimberly are still talking about the kids growing up. Joyce even mentions that she hopes Josh will try water skiing this year. Elaine then says, "I'm going to encourage Mark to give it a try this year, maybe that will be what it will take to encourage Josh." David then replies, "you know Josh, anything Mark is brave enough to try, Josh has to try."

Everyone decides to go up to the cabin and see what the boys are up to. Randy even mentions that they're probably watching t.v. So they get up and walk in. When they get in, they find the boys watching t.v. just like Randy guessed. Elaine then says, "why don't you boys go play outside for a while or something?" Tyler then replies, "like what?" Elaine thinks for a moment and Answers, "Joyce and I could move the cars out the way and you guys could play basketball."

The boys agree to Elaine's suggestion, so they go out to the garage and Mark gets the basketball. Joyce and Elaine move the cars and go back in the cabin. Mark then asks, "should we get a game of around the world going?" The other boys agree, and Mark starts the game. After Scott pulls off a surprising victory, the boys decide on a game of horse and Scott starts the game.

Tyler wins the game of horse and then Randy yells for the boys to come back in for dinner. Mark puts away the basketball and the boys walk back in the cabin. Once in, they find Kimberly sitting in a booster chair at the table. Then Joyce informs them that while they were playing basketball, someone had called her claiming they found Buster and sent her a text message with a picture of the dog they found, unfortunately it wasn't Buster.

The boys go and wash up and sit down at the dinner table. Randy puts a plate of steaks on the table and Joyce and Elaine bring out the rest of the food. David leads everyone in saying the dinner prayer and everyone starts eating. Mark then asks, "what are we doing after dinner?" David answers, "we thought maybe we could shoot off some bottle rockets and firecrackers. Then you kids could play with some sparklers."

After dinner everyone goes outside. Joyce and Elaine move the cars back in the driveway, while David and Randy get the fireworks they talked about lighting off. Joyce and Elaine light sparklers for the boys while David and Randy shoot off bottle rockets and firecrackers. The boys laugh and giggle as they play with the sparklers. Joyce lights a sparkler for Kimberly and tries to help with it. Josh yells, "hey mom look at this." Joyce looks at him and says, "that's really pretty.", as he writes his name in the air. Randy and David fire off a few more bottle rockets and fire crackers, then everyone goes in to play some games.

The next day the boys are the last to wake up. As they get ready for breakfast, they ask where Randy and David are. Elaine tells them that they went out early to play golf. Joyce mentions that when the get back, Randy and David will take them out fishing. The boys get excited about going fishing and start eating breakfast.

After breakfast, the boys take turns getting ready to go out. Mark goes first and the rest watch cartoons on t.v. Then it's Josh's turn, followed by Tyler then Scott. They watch cartoons for another half hour and Randy and David return from their golf game. The boys get up and start getting their fishing gear ready. Once done with that, they go down to the dock and get in the fishing boat.

Randy and David join them in the boat and they head of to their secret fishing spot. Randy then asks, "who's going to catch the biggest fish?" All the boys yell, "me!" Then Randy says, "I'll give a dollar to the boy that catches the biggest fish." They arrive at their fishing spot and drop the anchor. Randy fills the live well with water and everyone casts out their fishing line.

5 minutes later, Scott's bobber goes under water really hard and he starts to reel in. David says, "it looks like Scott got the first fish." Just then, David's bobber goes under and David says, "looks like I'm next." Scott reels his in first and Josh helps him with the net. Randy then says,

"look at the size of that sunny, it's bigger than my hand." David then reels in a sunny just as big. They both put their fish in the live well.

Everyone is excited about the fish that was caught and continue fishing. Mark gets a very hard hit on his line, and starts to reel in hard. Randy yells, "don't give up son, you've got him." Josh helps Mark with the net and everyone gets excited when they see he had caught a large mouth bass.

"Looks like Mark got the big one so far", said David. After about a half an hour later Randy catches a northern. They fish for another hour and every has caught a fair share of fish. All together they caught 12 sun fish, 5 croppies, 1 largemouth bass, and 2 northern. Then they pull up the anchor and head back.

Once back at the cabin, everyone puts away the fishing gear and Randy gives Mark a dollar for catching the biggest fish. They take the fish out the live well and drain the water out. Randy and David start cleaning the fish for the fish fry and store it in the fridge.

The boys notice that while they were gone, Elaine and Joyce took Kimberly in town to go shopping. They ask Randy to move his car so they can play basketball. He does that and they get started on the game. First they start a game of around the world. About halfway into it, they're all getting hot in the baking hot sun. Mark recalls hearing that it's getting up in the low 90's. They decide to take their shirts off and continue with the game.

Josh wins the game and they decide to start a game of 2 on 2. Mark and Scott against Josh and Tyler. This time they bet that the winning team gets to sucker punch the losers in the arm. Mark and Scott win the game and know they can get Josh and Tyler back for last night's nipple twists. Josh and Tyler stand next to the garage door with their left arms facing the street. Mark punches Josh in the arm and Scott punches Tyler in the arm.

The boys get into discussing what they'll play next when Elaine, Joyce, and Kimberly return. Elaine tells the boys that it's now lunch time and they should wash up. So the boys pick up their shirts, go wash up and sit down at the patio table.

Randy places a plate of hamburgers on the table, and David sets a bowl of baked beans on the table. They all say grace and start eating. Then Randy asks, "who wants to go water skiing later?" Mark raises his hand and Josh says, "oh I guess I'll give it a try." Tyler and Scott shake their heads and say, "no." Joyce and Elaine both say they'll go.

Everyone finishes lunch, and the boys go in and change into their swimsuits. Joyce brings Kimberly in and helps her change into her swimsuit. When the boys come out of their room, Joyce asks them to take Kimberly down to the beach and keep an eye on her. They leave with her and Elaine and Joyce get ready to water ski.

Down at the beach, the boys set Kimberly down on the sand and she gets started making sand castles. The boys go in the water, but stay close to shore so they can keep an eye on her as Joyce asked. The boys grab a Frisbee and start playing with it. Everyone else now arrives at the beach, and the boys go out in deeper water. David and Randy get the boat ready while Joyce and Elaine get the water skies ready.

Randy then asks, "who wants to go first?" Josh then answers, "I guess I will give it a try and get it over with." Josh puts on a life jacket and Joyce helps him with the water skies. David throws the rope to Josh and he gets ready. Once everyone is ready, Josh yells, "hit it!" The boat gets going, starts to pull Josh up. He moves about 20 feet and falls. They try everything again and this time Josh gets up. He skies for about 10 minutes and goes in. Everyone congratulates Josh on doing well. Then Mark says, "I'm next." Mark puts on a lifejacket and the water skies and Elaine helps him get ready.

As soon as Mark says he's ready, David tosses him the rope. Mark yells, "hit it." The boat gets up right away and everyone watches Mark water ski. Mark also goes about 10 minutes and goes in. Elaine tells him what a good job he did, then Joyce gets ready. While Joyce is water skiing, she releases her right ski and goes the rest of the time on one ski. Then it's Elaine's turn and she also goes on 1 ski.

After David and Randy water ski, they put the boat away. The boys continue rough housing. Randy and David get on air mattresses. Joyce puts a lifejacket on Kimberly and lets her swim in the area. Then Joyce and Elaine get on an air mattress and join David and Randy. After a couple hours, the pontoon parade goes by, and everyone sits in the water and watches. After the parade, everyone gets out, dries off, and goes in the cabin.

Everyone changes back in to regular clothes and relax by watching a movie. The boys put a blanket on the floor in front of the t.v. Then they grab some pillows and lie down on the floor. Joyce and Elaine make 2 big bowl of popcorn. One for the kids, and one for the adults. Everyone grabs a can of pop and the kids return to their spot on the floor and the adults sit on the couch or a chair. Mark pops a disc in the player and they all watch the movie.

After the movie, the kids go out and play, then Randy and David get started on the fish fry. Joyce and Elaine work on making salad for dinner. Once the salad is made, they go on to cut up the watermelon into small pieces. Elaine opens the kitchen window and yells for the kids to come in and eat.

The kids run in, wash up and sit down to eat. Elaine brings out the salad and everyone gets started. Then David gets the fish and French fries. Everyone enjoys a great meal.

After having fun at dinner time, the boys go out to the garage and get the fireworks. Then they set everything up for the fireworks show on the beach for later that evening. David and Randy gather up firewood for a campfire. Once all that is ready they get into playing games.

The sun starts to set late in the evening and Randy starts the campfire. Everyone sits around the campfire and the start to roast marshmallows and making s'mores. The kids get into telling jokes and everyone has lots of laughs. Then Mark starts singing his fart song. Mark sings, "there once was a man who farts allot, (makes fart noise), farts allot, (makes fart noise), farts allot, (makes fart noise), he farts all day long." The rest of the boys get laughing, then Elaine asks him to stop.

It finally gets dark and Randy and David get started on the fireworks show. They start things off with a couple of roman candles, then some of the bigger stuff. Everyone is amazed how pretty the fireworks are. All around the lake people are lighting off fireworks and enjoying a good show.

Once the fireworks are over, Mark grabs a flashlight and starts telling a ghost story while shining the light on his face. "There once was a man who was missing one hand. They say he used to live around here. He died one day, but his hand remained alive. They say his ghost went to live in his hand. His hand walked on it's fingers and walked around looking for who killed him."

Elaine interrupts, "don't make the story to scary honey, remember we have Kimberly here." Mark looks at her and says, "don't worry mom,

I tell this one all the time in the treehouse when Josh and Tyler are over for a sleepover and we sleep out. Elaine then tells him to continue.

Mark gets back into his story, "so this guy's hand is walking on it's fingers looking for his killer and doesn't find him right away. So he comes up with a plan. He remembered that the guy worked in a warehouse, and would be going to work on Monday. So this severed hand goes to the warehouse and waits. His killer shows up for work and goes straight to the forklift. He gets on and begins to move. The severed hand takes control of the forklift and moves it superfast. He then crashes it into a brick wall and a ton of bricks fall on his head and kills him. When he realizes he got his revenge he goes out and celebrates." Mark turns off the flashlight and sits down.

Elaine then says, "wow, what a story of revenge." Joyce looks at her watch and says, "it's now bedtime, let's go in and get ready for bed." They all get up and go in. The kids put on their pajamas, and say goodnight to everyone.

The next day, the kids get up and have breakfast. After they eat, they go and watch cartoons on t.v. for an hour. David then comes out with some garbage bags and asks the boys to go out to the beach with him and clean up. After they finish cleaning up the beach, they go in and play some board games.

After a few hours, Joyce announces that she and Elaine set up things for a scavenger hunt. She gives each boy a list of things to find and a pen to cross items of the list when they are found. The boys go outside and split up looking for things. The things they are to look for are, a bucket, a rock, a piece of wood, a glass bottle, a toothpick, a nail, and a mushroom.

The boys go out looking for the things on the list. They found the bucket down at the beach where Kimberly was making sand castles. Next was the rock a short distance from the bucket.

The boys continued their search. They went in the cabin and got a toothpick out the kitchen, then went back outside for the rest of the things. They found a twig that broke off a tree out in the yard. They put that in the bucket as the piece of wood they had to find. They went to the garbage can and in there they found a glass bottle. They went in the garage and found a nail on Randy's workbench. Mark was unsure as to where they could find a mushroom. They didn't buy any at the store, so they had to see if there was one growing somewhere. They looked for 20 minutes and found one growing in the yard near the lake. They picked it and put it in the bucket.

They brought the bucket with the other things in it in the cabin. Joyce and Elaine checked the things they found and saw they got everything on the list. They announce that it is now lunch time and they have some leftovers to eat. They all sit down and eat what they want.

After lunch the boys decide to go swimming. They change into their swimsuits, go outside and jump off the dock. Shortly after that, they get into roughhousing right away. An hour later everyone else comes out and they all take turns at water skiing. Once they finish water skiing, they relax for a while on air mattresses.

When they finish with swimming, they all get out the water and change back into regular clothes. They then clean up and pack. They then load up the cars and head off for home.

Mark and Scott wake up the next day and go outside. They climb up into their tree house and start planning for Kyle's initiation. Just then Josh and Tyler show up and ask if they can go up there. Mark asks them for the password. They both make armpit fart noises and Mark lets them in.

Josh asks Mark, "are you really going to let Kyle join the club?" Mark answers, "if we play our cards right, he'll refuse to join." Josh smiles and asks, "what kind of scheme do you have planned?" Mark answers, "we're planning it now." Josh grins and they all start thinking.

Mark then says, "I have an idea, we have a canoe paddle, and a tennis racket." Then Mark looks at Josh and asks, "do you have a ping pong paddle?" Josh answers, "yeah, we have one in the basement." Mark tells Josh to go home and get it. Then Mark asks Tyler, "do you have a hockey stick?" Tyler answers, "yeah I do." Mark tells him to go get it.

When Josh and Tyler return with their things, they climb up in the tree house and see that Mark and Scott have their things with them. Mark tells everyone stay in the tree house and he'll be right back. When Mark returns, he has a small bath towel in his hand. Everyone looks puzzled about why Mark brought a towel with him. Josh asks him, "what are these things for?" Mark replies, "oh you'll see, yeah you will see."

Mark then tells everyone to out of the tree house and look for a stick. They all found one stick each and brought it up to the tree house. Then they wait for Mark to tell them what they need next.

Mark then asks, "does anybody have any ideas as to what else we can do to Kyle?" Scott then answers, "we could throw water balloons at him." Mark smiles and replies, "that's a great idea Scott, I'll ride my bike to a nearby store to buy balloons later." Tyler then says, "hey I know, how about we make Kyle run an obstacle course." Mark then replies, "that's a great idea too. Now wait here while I get the balloons." Mark climbs down the treehouse and gets on his bike and heads for the store.

Up at the treehouse Josh, Tyler, and Scott are looking at the things they have and talk about them. Tyler asks, "what do you think Mark wants to do with the towel?" Scott answers, "I think he's going to get it wet, twirl it up like this, (demonstrates twirling) and whip it in Kyle's butt." Josh then replies, "no, it's too short. Mark will have to tell us when he gets back."

Just then Kyle shows up and yells up to the tree house, "are you guys ready for me yet?" Josh replies, "no, Mark isn't back yet, plus we have to set things up for you." Kyle asks, "when will that be?" Josh replies, "one of us will come and get you." Kyle waves goodbye and leaves.

After Kyle leaves, Josh turns to Scott and Tyler and asks them, "what are we going to do for an obstacle course?" Scott and Tyler get in to thinking for a short while then Scott says, "I bet we can set something up at the park, starting with those tires on the ground." Tyler then adds, "hey yeah, we can have him run through those." Then Mark returns and climbs up to the treehouse.

Mark opens a bag and shows everyone the balloons, then says, "we can get Kyle with these." Everyone is pleased with the amount of balloons Mark bought. They all get to wondering what else they are going to do so Mark puts away the balloons and grabs the bath towel.

"First we will blindfold Kyle with this, the we will make him walk on his hands and knees from this end of the yard to the other and back with each of smacking him on the butt with these things." (pointing to the canoe paddle, hockey stick, tennis racket, and ping pong paddle) Mark continues, "don't hit him too hard, we don't want to hurt him, just get him to quit."

Mark explains more about smacking Kyle in the butt. "I'll start with the canoe paddle, then Josh with the hockey stick, followed by

Tyler with the ping pong paddle, and finally Scott with the tennis rack. When Scott is done, I'll move to the front of the line and we start over again till Kyle gets to the end, then he turns around and we continue."

Josh then says, "that sounds like fun, but what about the sticks?" Mark explains, "with the sticks we play guess who hit you? We make him stand up, but keep his blindfold on and we take random turns hitting him in the butt, and he guesses who did it. Once he gets it right we stop."

Tyler then asks, "do we hit him with the water balloons next?" Mark answers, "yes, we keep the blindfold on him and we throw water balloons at his feet." Tyler then asks, "Do we go to the park for the obstacle course next?" Mark looks at Tyler and says, "you bet Tyler, and I know we can figure out a good course there." Scott then asks, "do you think he'll quit at this point?" Mark replies, "I'm not sure, but I have a surprise up my sleeve just in case."

Mark grabs the balloons and tells everyone to meet him over by the garden hose. They climb down and Mark runs in the garage and grabs a bucket and they all get together at the garden hose and fill the balloons with water and put them in the bucket.

Mark then tells everyone to wait in the back yard while he gets Kyle. Mark leaves and the rest of the boys go over to the patio and sit down. Tyler then says, "this is going to be great, making Kyle pay for all the mean things he did to us over the years." Josh then adds, "yeah, revenge is going to be sweet."

Mark arrives at Kyle's house and rings the doorbell. Kyle answers the door and Mark tells him to come over. Kyle walks out of the house and the two of them start walking toward Mark's house. Kyle then says, "I can't wait to join your club, I've been wanting to for some time now." Mark then adds, "Josh, Tyler, and Scott are looking forward to seeing you."

They arrive at Mark's house and go into the back yard. Mark instructs Josh and Tyler to get the things they need down from the treehouse. Kyle then asks, "hey, I was just thinking, has the police or anyone found anything on Buster yet?" Scott replies, "nothing yet, but we're hoping." Mark then adds, "I hear tips and leads come in every so often."

Josh and Tyler bring everything down that they need for Kyle's initiation. Kyle takes a look at the things they bring down, and his bottom jaw drops open. Kyle has a shocked look on his face and asks, "what do you need all this for?" Mark replies, "you must complete 5 test before you join our club. Don't worry, Josh and Tyler had to do the same thing." Kyle looks at Josh and Tyler and they are just smiling and nodding their heads.

Kyle looks at Mark like he's having 2nd thoughts about this. Then he says, "I thought you were going to swear me in on the bible or something." Mark replies, "that part comes later, 1st we have to get you to take these 5 tests.

Kyle agrees to the terms and Mark brings Kyle to the starting point of the 1st test. Josh hands Mark the towel and Mark gets ready to blindfold him. Mark then explains to Kyle that he has to get down on his hands and knees and crawl from one end of the yard to the other while blindfolded. Kyle declares, "that should be easy." Mark then tells him, "it gets tougher later."

Mark proceeds to blindfold Kyle. Josh then grabs his hockey stick, Tyler picks up the ping pong paddle and Scott picks up the tennis racket. Mark helps Kyle down to the ground and says, "When I tell you to start crawling, then you get started." Mark then picks up the canoe paddle.

Mark gets in line first, then Josh, Tyler, and Scott. Mark tells Kyle to go and he starts moving. Mark whacks Kyle 1st, then Josh, followed by Tyler and Scott. The boys follow Kyle and keep whacking him till he gets to the end of the yard. Mark then tells Kyle to turn around. He turns around and the boys continue their whacking.

When Kyle finishes crawling back to where he started, Mark helps him up and moves him to where test number 2 starts. Mark then says, "congratulations, you passed the 1st test. Now on to test number 2. We're going to play guess who hit you." The boys put away the items from the first test and pick up their sticks.

The boys then then stand in a spot surrounding Kyle and Mark says, "now each of us is going to take a random turn hitting you, then you have to guess who hit you." Mark points to Scott and Scott hits Kyle. After he is hit, Kyle guesses, "um, I think that was Tyler." Mark tells him he's wrong and points to Josh. He aims low and hits Kyle, then Kyle says, "I think that was Scott." Once again Mark tells him that he's wrong.

The boys begin to smile because they get to keep going. Mark signals that he's next and takes his turn. Kyle guesses Josh and is told that he's wrong. Tyler takes his turn and Kyle guesses Scott. Josh informs Kyle that everyone has hit him once. Scott takes a turn and Kyle guesses Mark. Now he is told he is wrong for a 5th time and Kyle is frustrated.

Mark takes a turn and Kyle guesses Tyler, but is informed that he is wrong. Kyle then says, "I hope you're not lying to me." Tyler replies, "I promise we're not." Scott takes a turn and Kyle guesses Scott. Mark then says, "congratulations, you got it right." The boys put down their sticks and Mark leads him to the water balloons.

Mark informs Kyle he passed test number 2, and that test number 3 will begin. Mark picks up the bucket and they all take 2 each and start throwing them at Kyles feet. Kyle jumps each time a balloon bursts and water splashes on him. Josh and Mark take the last 2 balloon out the bucket and throw them at his feet. Mark announces, "that's the end of test 3." He then takes the blindfold off and Kyle dries himself off with it.

Kyle then asks, "so what do you guys have planned next?" Tyler answers, "now we go to the park and you run through our obstacle course." Kyle then says, "you sure make it tough to join your club." Scott replies with, "we have to, because we can't let just anybody in." The boys then head off to the park.

On the way to the park, they meet up with Ryan Benson, the older brother of Katie and Jessica. Ryan asks, "where are you going?" Josh answers, "we're taking Kyle to the park for his treehouse initiation." Josh winks his eye and Ryan catches on to what's going on.

Ryan looks at Kyle and says, "I wish the best of luck to you Kyle." The boys look a little nervous that Ryan might blow the deal, then Kyle says, "thank you Ryan." Then Ryan adds, "I also hear my kid sister, Jessica has a crush on Tyler." Mark and Josh laugh while Tyler's face turns red. Tyler replies, "shut up Ryan!!!!!!!!" The other boys giggle quietly, then Ryan says, "o.k. chill out dude."

The boys arrive at the park and Ryan asks, "do you mind if I stay and watch Kyle go through this?" Mark answers, "go right ahead." The boys go right to where the tires are. Mark tells Kyle, "this is where it all begins." Kyle looks at the tires and says, "I guess you want me to run through these like they do in the Army?" Mark answers, "yeah, that's right."

Kyle hen asks, "so then what?" Mark replies, "we haven't figured out that yet, but I guess you can run to that wall, and climb the rope, ring the bell and climb down. Then run to the merry go round (they walk to the merry go round) and we will spin it, you get on here, walk through and get off here, run to the seesaw where Ryan will sit on one side and you on the other, ride it up and down 5 times, get off and do 10 push-ups."

Mark then asks, "do you have any questions?" Kyle answers, No, I'm ready to get started." All but Ryan walk back to the tires, while Ryan gets ready on the seesaw. Kyle gets in starting position and Mark says, "ready, set, go!" Kyle gets running through the tires and almost falls over half way.

Next he runs to the wall, grabs a hold of the rope and places his feet tight on the bottom of the wall. Then he starts to climb up. He struggles a couple of times, but makes it up and rings the bell. He climbs down and everyone is amazed that he made it this far.

Everyone runs to the merry go round and starts it spinning. Kyle jumps on and rests for a short moment. Then Kyle tries to make it across to the other side. With the merry go round in motion, he waits till he's on the right side and jumps off. Once off, he runs to the seesaw.

He gets on the seesaw with Ryan and rides it up and down 5 times. Then he gets off and does 10 push-ups. Kyle stands up and Mark says, "congratulations, you're almost done. Kyle smiles and says, "I can't wait to join your club. Josh, Tyler, and Scott look worried. Scott whispers to Tyler, "I sure hope Mark knows what he is doing." Tyler nods his head.

Mark then asks Kyle, "are you ready to go back to my house for the 5th and final test?" Kyle replies, "give me a couple minutes to catch my breath." Mark then says, "sure, we can wait."

After a couple minutes, Kyle is rested up and says, "o.k. I'm ready, let's go back to your house Mark for the final test." The boys head off and Ryan says, "I have to run home for a moment, but let me know how everything turns out." Mark then replies, "yeah we will." Ryan leaves and the rest of the boys continue on.

The boys get half way to Mark's house and then they are spotted by Katie and Jessica. Tyler pretends he doesn't see Jessica. Scott then says, "hey Tyler, isn't that your girlfriend?" Tyler answers, "shut up or I'll beat you up." Katie asks, "what are you guys doing with Kyle?" Josh answers, "we're putting Kyle through the treehouse initiation. Kyle then

adds, "yeah, and I'm almost done, just one more test and I'm a member."
The girls leave and the boys walk into the back yard.

Once in the back yard, Mark instructs everyone to wait for him. He
goes in the house and they wait.

Mark goes in the kitchen and looks inside the refrigerator. Elaine
walks by and asks, "what are you looking for honey?" Mark looks up at
his mother and thinks up a lie then answers, "I'm looking for a snack for
me and the guys." Elaine then replies, "don't eat too much, we're eating
dinner in a few hours." She walks off and Mark continues looking.

Finally, Mark finds a half pint of tartar sauce. He smiles and pulls it
out of the fridge. He then grabs wooden spoon from a kitchen drawer.
He finds a brown paper bag under the sink near the garbage and puts
the tartar sauce and wooden spoon in the bag. Having everything he
wanted, goes back outside in the back yard. He then instructs the others
to meet him by the treehouse.

Mark has Kyle stand about 2 ½ feet from the ladder going up in
the treehouse. Then he has the rest of the guys stand a few feet behind
Kyle. Then Mark says, "Stay here, and keep your head facing the tree.
Now close your eyes, and we will complete test 5. Kyle thinks to himself,
"finally, I'm going to be a member of the club."

Mark climbs up in the treehouse with the bag of things he brought
out of the house and then says, "o.k., keep your eyes closed and your
head facing the tree." Mark then takes everything out of the bag. He
opens up the pint of tartar sauce and grabs the wooden spoon. He
scoops out half the tartar sauce and dumps it on Kyle's head.

Kyle opens his eyes and realizes what just happened. Then he says,
"oh gross! That's it, I quit!" Then he runs off. The other boys laugh
in delight. Josh then says, "well, I guess we showed him." Mark climbs
down and declares, "I guess we showed him."

The boys get to thinking that it's time to celebrate. Just then they
hear the sound of an ice cream truck going down the street. They all
get the same idea and check their pockets for money. They all find that
they have enough to buy something. They run to the ice cream truck
and wait in line.

Mark is 1st to get his order and he gets an ice cream sandwich. Josh
is next and buys a chocolate sundae. Tyler orders a chocolate cone and
finally Scott orders a vanilla cone. The boys walk back to the back yard
and sit down in the patio eating their ice cream treats.

Josh then asks Mark, "where did you get the idea for dumping tartar sauce on Kyle's head?" Mark smiles and says, "you remember when I told Kyle there was something fishy about him wanting to join our club?" Josh laughs and replies, "Oh I get it." Mark remembers that he left everything in the tree house, runs up there and grabs the tartar sauce and the wooden spoon, goes in the house puts everything away and returns to the patio.

The boys get to thinking about playing some basketball so they walk to Josh and Tyler's house. They get a game of 2 against 2 going. Mark and Scott against Josh and Tyler. They play 1st team to 20 points wins the game. Mark and Scott win by a score of 20-17. Just then David returns home from work and Mark and Scott start going home.

David tells his boys to clean up for dinner. Josh and Tyler walk in and clean up. David cleans a few things in the driveway then walks in. The boys walk out of the bathroom and David says, "boys let's go eat dinner and then I can tell you my good news." They sit down at the dining room table just as Joyce is finishing putting dinner on the table.

Everyone dishes up and starts eating. Then David says, "Joyce, Josh, Tyler, and Kimberly, guess what?" Everyone looks at David and asks, "what?" Seeing the excitement in everybody, David says, "You my friend John who works at the pound?" Josh replies, "yeah dad, we know him." David continues, "well he called me today and reported that they just got a German Shepard that looks like Buster and we can have it for free.

Everyone at the table was suddenly silent. Then Tyler says, "but dad, we don't want another dog, we want Buster." David replies, "I understand that, but what if Buster never comes home? I of surly want Buster back too, but let's be realistic, chances are he won't." Nobody says anything for a few seconds then David continues, "we don't have to make a decision now, but I have to call John back in 3 days.

Meanwhile Mark and Scott return home. When they walk in the house, they see Elaine isn't very happy. Elaine then says, "I just got a call from Kyle Smith's mother, what do you know about dumping tartar sauce in Kyle's hair?" Mark and Scott freeze in their tracks, knowing that they're in trouble.

Elaine looks straight at Mark and Scott and tells them, "I know you guys did it, I checked the tartar sauce in the fridge and half of it is missing. I also noticed the wooden spoon covered with tartar sauce in the dishwasher." Mark and Scott both look sad, then Elaine continues, "so what do you have to say for yourselves?" Mark replies, "I'm sorry mom, it was just a prank." Elaine looking disappointed with them points to the stairs and says, "go up and wash up for dinner, we will talk about your punishment later." The boys walk upstairs mumbling to themselves about what's going to happen to them.

Mark and Scott wash up wondering if their dad knows what happened. They also start questioning what their mother is going to do to them. Scott looks at Mark and says, "mom really sounded mad." Mark finishes washing his hands and says, "yeah I guess we really did it this time." The boys then head downstairs for dinner.

They all sit down at the dinner table and Mark asks, "hey, where's dad? Isn't he back from Minneapolis?" Elaine replies, "no he got called to take a flight to Houston, he'll be home tomorrow." They all finish eating then Elaine says, I decided to make your punishment one I think is fair, you're both grounded the next couple of days." Mark and Scott agree to the punishment and head up to their room.

CHAPTER

9

There was a severe thunder storm warning in the Deerfield, IL area just a few days after Mark and Scott were done being grounded. The storm had frequent lightning strikes and pea to marble size hail. Randy looks out the window and is glad he doesn't have a flight that morning. The phone rings and Elaine answers.

While Elaine is talking on the phone, Randy, Mark and Scott are watching weather reports on t.v. The meteorologist on t.v. is reporting heavy rain and hail going through Deerfield and Northbrook. He says, "The storm going through Deerfield right now is slowly moving north east. There is however another system behind it, and this one possess the threat of generating a tornado."

Elaine gets off the phone and sits next to Randy as they continue watching the weather reports on t.v. The storm calms down for a while, but they are reminded of wave 2 will go through in about 10 minutes. A report comes in that a weather observer is seeing rotation in a cloud and suspects a tornado could land in or near Deerfield.

Meanwhile at the Hanson's house, Joyce is comforting Kimberly. Tyler says, "what a baby." Joyce then replies, "well you do have to remember, she is only 3 years old. Plus, I remember last summer, a storm like this went through here, and you got so scared you ran upstairs and hid under your bed." Tyler replies, "well I was just a kid then."

A couple of big lightning strikes hit nearby and Kimberly yells, "Mommy!" Joyce holds her a little closer and tells her everything is going to be o.k.

The Air Raid Sirens sound. David turns on a radio that he keeps in the living room. They all listen and hear a weather report that there is a tornado on the ground 5 miles north east of Deerfield. It is also reported that the tornado is moving east at about 30 m.p.h.

Josh then says, "I hope Buster is all right." David then turns down the volume on the radio and says, "I hope so too Josh, but we don't even know if he is still alive." Joyce then adds, "not to mention, we don't know where he is." There is a loud crash of thunder, Then David says, "oh by the way guys, I talked to my friend John, he still has that other German Shepherd that we can have for free. He can allow us only 3 more days, then he has to sell it."

Back at the Miller's house, Randy turns off the t.v. as the storm starts to let up. Elaine then says, "oh by the way, that was Joyce Hanson I was talking to on the phone. She says were all invited to their house tomorrow for a pool party." Everyone gets excited and Randy says, "Great! I have the next couple of days off, so this makes perfect timing for me."

"What time are we supposed to be there?", asks Mark. Elaine answers, "5 p.m. and we're having dinner there too." Randy then asks, "Should we bring anything?" Elaine replies, "David is going to grill burgers, Joyce is going to make her baked beans and she wants you to make your world famous potato salad, and I should bake one apple and one cherry pie." Randy then smiles and says, sounds like fun deer."

Mark and Scott look out the window and notice the storm is starting to lighten up. They get up and go upstairs. Then they get into thinking about what to do while waiting for the storm to end.

They then get out their video games and start playing. Mark then says, "that sure was a wild storm, even a tornado came down north east of here." Scott then replies, "yeah, that was a close one." They play their games for a half hour and then the sun starts to shine.

Elaine walk in the room and says to Mark and Scott, "we're going outside to clean up, you two beter come and help." Mark and Scott turn off their games and put them away. They go out and get started cleaning up. They look 3 houses down the street and see Josh and Tyler doing the same.

People in the neighborhood get into talking about how bad the storm was. Randy takes a good look at the house to see if there was any hail damage. He didn't find any. After cleaning both front and back yards, Mark and Scott went into their treehouse to see if anything happened. They were delighted to see that only the chairs got knocked over, and the table moved out of place.

Once clean-up was done, Mark and Scott went to see how Josh and Tyler were doing. When they arrived at Josh and Tyler's house, they found that Josh and Tyler had just finished up. Josh then says, "that was some storm. Did you guys have a lot of cleaning up to do?" Mark replies, "yeah we had a lot back home too. Plus, we had to straighten up the table and chairs in the tree house."

The boys got into playing a game of basketball. Josh and Tyler won this time. Mark then says, "that was fun, but if we play you guys tomorrow at the pool party, Scott and I will cream you." Both Josh and Tyler start laughing. Then Josh says, "yeah right Mark, dream on." Scott then replies, "don't be so sure of yourselves, we've won games against you before." David then walks up to the boys and tells Josh and Tyler that they have to leave and go to grandma's house. Mark and Scott say good bye and leave.

Mark and Scott return Home. They find Randy in the family room watching t.v. and Elaine in the living room reading the newspaper. Elaine asks, "did you have a fun time at Josh and Tyler's?" Mark answers, "yeah it was fun." Elaine says, "that's nice." Mark and Scott head upstairs.

As soon as they get upstairs, the phone rings and Mark answers it in his parent's bedroom. "Hello?", says Mark. It turns out to be Ryan Benson and he asks how things went with Kyle. Mark then says, "yeah, I guess I forgot to call you. I ended up dumping tartar sauce on his head and he quit. Scott and I got grounded after words."

Ryan then asks Mark if they could meet at the park later. Mark checks with his mom and she tells him o.k. Mark tells Ryan he and Scott will be there in 15 minutes. He hangs up the phone and he goes in his bedroom with Scott.

"What did Ryan want?", asks Scott. "He wants us to meet him at the park, and bring your baseball glove, we might get a game started later with some other guys.", answered Mark. Scott picks up his baseball glove, then Mark picks up his, and the 2 say goodbye to their parents as they walk out the front door.

When they get to they get to the park, they go straight to the ball field. There they find Ryan, half his team mates, and 4 other guys from his neighborhood. They choose up sides with Ryan and some of the guys on his team, and the rest on Mark and Scott's team. Then they get a game started with Ryan's team at bat first. Ryan's team wins the game 4-3.

After the game, Mark and Scott shake hands with Ryan and tell him they had a great time. Then they walk home.

The next day, Mark and Scott wake up with excitement. They get out of bed wearing only their underwear. They jump around the room as they glad this is the day of the pool party. They get so loud that Randy walks in and asks them to quiet down, because he and Elaine are still trying to sleep.

Scott is first dressed then Mark. They head down stairs, and get started on breakfast. Elaine is next to walk in the kitchen, then Randy. The boys continue with their excitement, because all they can think about is all the fun they are going to have at the pool party. Elaine then says, "I wish you boys would get that excited about getting good grades in school."

Mark and Scott finish breakfast and put their dishes away. They then go out and play. They start out on the swings and have jumping of the swings contest, followed by a contest to see who can swing the highest. After an hour, Elaine came out to talk to the boys. She said, "boys, come and get in the car. We have to go to the store and get somethings for the pool party."

Mark and Scott quit playing and get in the car. Elaine gets in the front passenger seat. Randy gets in and starts driving. They get moving down the main road and Randy starts whistling to the song playing on the radio. Elaine joins in with singing along. Mark and Scott look at each other and laugh because they think their parents have gone off the deep end.

They arrive at the grocery store and get out of the car. Mark and Scott continue their laughing at Randy and Elaine. Then Elaine says, "o.k. you boys had your fun, now settle down and let's get in the store. The boys quit laughing and walk in with Randy and Elaine.

Elaine grabs cart and they walk into the produce section first. Randy grabs some potatoes and puts them in the cart. Elaine puts a bag of apples and some cherries in the cart. Right about that time, Joyce and David enter in with their kids. Kimberly is riding in the cart. Josh and Tyler are walking along side with them.

Randy and Elaine continue putting things they need in their cart. Mark and Scott look back and see Josh and Tyler. Mark then says, "hey mom and dad, Josh and Tyler are here." Randy and Elaine look back and see them. Elaine looks at Mark and says, "it looks like they got the same idea we did."

Joyce and David move through the store picking up the things they need. Then Josh notices Mark and Scott in the store and says, "hey mom there's Mark and Scott." David and Joyce look up and see Randy and Elaine. Joyce then says, "well obviously, they have to get somethings for the pool party too." David and Joyce continue shopping.

A few minutes later, the 2 families bump into each other. Joyce then says, "wow! We must be thinking of the same thing. Are you also buying things for the pool party?" Elaine answers, "I guess great minds think alike, yes this is for the pool party." Joyce looks in Elaine's shopping cart, points to a few things in the cart and asks, "is that the stuff for your secret potato salad?" Randy answers, "never you mind Joyce, besides that is only part of it."

Joyce then laughs and says, "o.k. we won't bother you any more, we'll see you at the pool party." Elaine replies, "yeah, it should be fun." The 2 families go their own way. Randy and Elaine finish their shopping, and get in the check-out line. The cashier starts to ring things up as Mark and Scott are looking at candy bars. Randy tells Mark and Scott to leave the candy bars alone.

Randy pays for the groceries they bought, and they all make their way to the door. Mark and Scott look back for a moment and see Josh and Tyler getting in the check-out line with their parents. They wave goodbye to Josh and Tyler, then Josh and Tyler wave back.

When Randy and Elaine get home with the boys, Randy gets started on making his potato salad while Elaine gets started baking pies. Mark and Scott put everything else away, then go out and play.

The phone rings and Elaine answers. She gets into talking to her mother while Randy continues making his potato salad. Randy gets frustrated, because he can't find the mustard. Elaine opens the fridge door and hands him the mustard, then gets back into talking to her mom.

Randy finishes up making his potato salad and leaves the kitchen. While talking on the phone, Elaine continues with the pies. She finishes with them, and puts them in the oven. Elaine says goodbye to her mother and hangs up the phone. She then walks out of the kitchen and enters the living room.

Elaine sits on the couch with Randy. Elaine then says, "I was just talking to mother, as usual she worries if her grandchildren are eating enough." Randy asks, "did you tell her about the pool party?" Elaine then answers, "yeah, I told her that. She still worries though." Randy then replies, "well now you know what to worry about when we have grandchildren." They both laugh.

At 4:30 p.m. Randy and Elaine start getting ready for the pool party. They tell Mark and Scott to go and put on their swimsuits while they get the food finished up and ready.

Mark and Scott, after changing their clothes, walk down stairs wearing a swimsuit, shirt, and sandals. Elaine sees them and says, "wow, you guys look great." Randy takes a look at them and says, "I agree, you guys are both ready for a pool party." Randy puts some ice in a cooler, he and Elaine put in the food and add more ice.

Elaine says to the boys, "why don't you 2 go up to the hall closet and grab 2 beach towels and then we will leave shortly." Mark and Scott do that, while Randy and Elaine pack a small bag with sunscreen and sunglasses take with. Mark and Scott walk down with their beach towels, and Elaine says, "I think we're ready, let's go out and have fun."

While walking on the way, Scott asks, "hey dad, do think the Hanson's will ever get Buster back?" Randy answers, "I don't know son, it looks grim, I hear they might settle for this other dog they have at the pound." Scott then replies, "that's too bad, I really liked Buster."

They arrive at the Hanson's house and walk right into the backyard. When they arrive, David is just firing up the grill. Josh and Tyler are already in the pool. Kimberly is playing in her sandbox. Joyce is sitting in a lawn chair watching the kids. David says, "Hi Randy and Elaine, I'm glad you and the kids are here." Josh yells, "hey Mark and Scott, get in, the water is nice and warm."

Randy sets the cooler down on the ground next to the picnic table. Then he and Elaine sit down in lawn chairs. Mark and Scott both take off their shirts and sandals. Then Elaine puts sunscreen on both of them. Mark and Scott then run and jump in the pool, and start rough housing with Josh and Tyler. David then goes in the house to get the burger patties.

Kimberly gets out of her sandbox and walks over to Joyce and says, "mommy, where's my big red shovel?" Joyce answers, "don't you remember? You broke it last month and we had to throw it away." Kimberly says, "oh yeah." She then turns and goes back to her sandbox.

David comes out of the house with a plate full of burger patties and places it on the picnic table and sits down on a lawn chair. Meanwhile the boys decide to have a cannon ball jumping contest. They get out and Josh goes first, then Tyler, followed by Mark then Scott. Josh proclaims, "I won!" Mark replies, "oh yeah?", and the boys start rough housing again.

David grabs a beer out of his cooler and asks Randy if he wants one. Randy Says, "yeah, sure. I'm not flying for a couple of days." David hands Randy a beer and asks, "ladies?" Joyce answers, "no thanks honey, I'm going to have some iced tea that I made. How about you Elaine?" After a short while, Elaine answers, "yeah, iced tea sounds good to me too." Joyce pours out 2 glasses of iced tea and gives one to Elaine.

The boys decide to have a chicken fight. Tyler gets up on Josh's shoulders and Scott gets up on Mark's. The chicken fight begins and Tyler starts out with a slight upper hand. After a while, Scott gets the upper hand. Tyler and Scott start to yell at each other, and calling each other names. In the end, Scott finally knocks Tyler in the water.

David gets out of his chair, scraps off the grill with a grill brush then puts the burger patties on the grill. David and Randy move their chairs over by the grill so they can watch the burgers while the talk about sports and drink beer. Meanwhile Elaine and Joyce get into talking about the kids.

The boys get into taking turns jumping off the diving board. They do cannon balls, dives and Mark even does a belly flop. After a belly flop, Mark yells "ow! That hurt!" Josh then replies, "what do you expect when you do a belly flop, you goof?" Mark answers, "at least I didn't do that of the high dive at the city pool." The boys continue their diving.

Kimberly gets out of her sandbox and walks over to David. She asks, "how much longer till we eat daddy?" David answers, "another 15 or 20 minutes, I just put the burgers on a few minutes ago." Kimberly walks back to her sandbox and continues playing. David and Randy resume talking about baseball.

After a while, David announces that the burgers are almost done. Joyce walks over to the sandbox, picks up Kimberly, and brings her in to wash her off. The boys get out of the pool, dry themselves off, then walk in the house to wash their hands. The boys sit at the picnic table in their swimwear so they can swim after words.

Everyone else cleans off and sits down. They say a prayer and start eating. Josh and Mark have a burping contest while Tyler and Scott laugh at them burping. They question who is the loudest. Randy looks at the boys and says, "you guys and your silly contests." All 4 boys laugh with a very wild laugh.

After everyone is done eating, the boys leave the picnic table and jump in the pool. The rest get going on clean up. When everyone is done cleaning up, David and Randy sit down in their chairs and talk about sports. Joyce and Elaine sit down with Kimberly and talk some more about the kids. Josh gets out of the pool, walks over to the diving board and says, "hey mom watch me dive." Joyce and Elaine look at Josh as he dives in. When he is done, Joyce claps her hands and says, "that was good honey."

Meanwhile across the street, Kyle is in his bedroom looking out the window and watching the pool party. He grumbles to himself, "nobody ever invites me to a pool party." He sees all the fun everyone is having and grumbles, "maybe I should crash this party and ruin their fun." He walks away from the window and moves to his dresser and pulls his swim suit out.

Kyle puts his swim suit on and a pair of sandals on. Then he grabs a beach towel from the hall closet. He looks at himself in the bathroom mirror and thinks he needs one more thing. He returns to his bedroom and puts on a pair off sunglasses. He takes one last look in the mirror and thinks he looks cool.

He walks out the front door, then runs across the street yelling, "yay! Yippee! Pool party!" Just as Kyle enters the back yard, he takes off his shirt and waves it over his head. Joyce sees him enter, gets out of her chair, walks over to him and gets a hold of him. She asks, "where do you think you're going?" Kyle answers, "to join the pool party."

Joyce gets a little disgusted and says, "wrong, you weren't invited. If you weren't so busy bullying the neighborhood kids, I'd consider letting you come. Now turn around and go home." Kyle puts his shirt back on and starts walking home. He thinks to himself, "they'll love me again when I play my trump card." Joyce turns, walks back to her chair and sits down.

Randy then says to David, "you always kept the gate padlocked shut, why haven't you bought a new lock yet?" David answers, "you know me, I'm such a procrastinator." Randy smiles and says, "yeah, if it weren't for Elaine, half my honey do list would never get done." The 2 men laugh and high five each other. Randy says, "here's to horse whipped men."

Randy sips some of his beer and says, "I was just thinking, I wonder if the police over looked something when they checked things for any clues that could lead to the arrest of Buster's kidnapper." David replies, "let's go over their now and take a closer look." The 2 men get up and walk over to where the gate is.

Randy takes a closer look at the broken padlock. Then he says, "look at this, I just found a small bloodstain on the back of the lock." David takes a closer look at the padlock and sees the bloodstain. Both Randy and David agree that this should be reported to the police.

After calling the police, David and Randy return to their chairs. Randy then says, "maybe now we can find out who kidnapped Buster." David replies, "yeah, and he can go to jail where he belongs." David and Randy both pick up their beer bottles and click their bottles together. Then both of them say, "justice at last."

The Police show up at the house about 15 minutes after David calls them. Across the street, Kyle is worried that the cops are looking for him for crashing the party, so he hides in the basement. David and Randy walk out to meet the cops. The first officer introduces himself as Officer O'Brian of the Deerfield crime lab. The 2nd officer introduces himself as Officer Jackson.

They all walk over to the Gate and David shows Officer O'Brian the blood stain on the padlock. Officer O'Brian takes a look at the padlock and says, "we would like to take this with us to the crime lab to analyze it. It might even serve as evidence to convict whoever did this." David agrees and Officer O'Brian puts the padlock in a plastic bag. David and Randy shake hands with both officers, then the 2 cops leave.

David and Randy Return to the back yard and return to their seats. Joyce is wondering why the cops where there. She asks David and he explains everything. Elaine then says, "wow, is that something. Now maybe we will find out who did this."

The boys finish their swimming and get out the pool and dry off. Randy then says, "I suppose we better get going." The boys finish drying themselves off and put on their shirts and sandals. Elaine and Randy put left overs in their cooler and close the lid. They all say good bye and leave.

On the way home, Scott asks Randy, "is it true You and David found a clue to who kidnapped Buster Dad?" Randy answers, "yes it's true, we found a small blood stain on the padlock." Mark then replies, "wow! I sure hope this proves who did it."

CHAPTER

10

The next day, Mark gets a phone call from Josh while he and Scott are eating breakfast. They get invited over for some more swimming in the pool. Mark asks Elaine if they can go, and She informs him they have to wait till after lunch. Mark gets off the phone with Josh, and he and Scott get excited about going swimming again.

Meanwhile, at the Hanson's house Josh and Tyler are making plans for when Mark and Scott come over. Josh says to Tyler, "we have to make plans for when Mark and Scott come over." Tyler adds, "yeah, like have the ultimate chicken fight and the ultimate basketball game." Josh then replies, "now you're thinking brother." The 2 then hi five each other.

Back at the Miller's house, Elaine is vacuuming the living room. When she is finished, she puts away the vacuum cleaner. She then calls for Mark and Scott. They enter the room and she says, "boys, get in the car. We have to go shopping for your cousin Jackie. It's her 9th birthday this Saturday.

Mark looks sad and says, "aw mom, Jackie is so weird. She thinks Martians live in her back yard." Elaine replies, "don't aw mom me, as weird as you think she is, we're shopping for her birthday. Now get in the car." The boys and Elaine go out in the garage and get in the car.

The boys are quiet the whole way to the store. They really don't like shopping for Jackie. All they can think about is the crazy stories about the Martians in her back yard. Then there's those weird glasses she wears that make her look ugly. They just know this shopping trip won't be any fun. On the way there, both Mark and Scott feel like they are walking their last mile.

They arrive at the store and get out of the car. Mark whispers to Scott, "at least it's a toy store so we can think up ideas for our future birthdays on the side." Scott smiles as they enter the store. Elaine grabs a shopping cart as they walk in. She then walks straight to where the girl toys are and says, "let's split up, you 2 boys look over there (points to her right) and I'll look around here."

The boys walk off and look around in their area. When Elaine isn't looking, they sneak off to the boy's section to look for some things for themselves they might want. Then they return back to the girl's section to look for a gift for Jackie.

Elaine calls for the boys and they run to where she is. When they get to where she is, they see her holding up a doll of a little girl wearing pink glasses. Elaine then asks, "what do you guys think of this as a gift for Jackie?" Mark answers, "that's perfect, it even looks a lot like Jackie." Elaine puts the doll in the cart, then they go and look for a card for Jackie.

They walk over to where the gift cards are and start reading. Scott starts to laugh and hands Elaine a card saying, "hey mom read this, it's funny." Elaine reads the card Scott hands her and reads it. She laughs and says, "that's a good one Scott, we'll get it."

They walk over to the check-out line. Elaine puts both items on the conveyer belt. After paying for everything, Elaine asks, "how would you guys like to have lunch at that ice cream parlor you both like?" Mark and Scott both get excited and Elaine says, "I'll take that as a yes." Elaine and the boys then walk out the door and head off to the car. They get in the car and Mark insists on the radio being played loud on their favorite station.

They arrive at the ice cream parlor, and sit down at a table near the front of the building. A waitress walks up to them, hands them each a menu and says, "my name is Jane, I'll be your server today. I'll be back in a few minutes to take your order." She walks off and Elaine, Mark, and Scott look at the menus.

Jane returns after a few minutes and asks, "are you ready to order?" Elaine answers, "I'll have the chef's salad and iced tea." Mark places his order, "I'll have a bacon cheese burger with fries and milk." Then Scott places his order, "I'll have the fish and chips with milk." Jane takes the menus and says, "o.k. I'll go place your order." Then she walks off.

Elaine then asks, "so what's going on with Josh and Tyler today?" Mark answers, "we're just going swimming over there today." Elaine replies, "I hear David is going to call his friend at the pound today, and they'll be getting a new dog." Scott then adds, "I wish they were getting Buster back instead." Elaine then says, "so do I, but I'm afraid we need a miracle." Mark then adds, "maybe we'll get one."

Jane returns with the food and says, "that's a chef's salad and iced tea for you miss, bacon cheese burger with fries and milk for you sir and fish and chips with milk for you sir. Will there be anything else?" Elaine answers, "not right now, thanks." Jane walks off.

Everyone begins to eat their food. After a short while, Mark says, "I wonder if the police will find who did it, now that they found that bloodstain on the padlock." Elaine replies, "I hope so too, but keep in mind, that could take weeks." They eat some more of their food, then Scott says, "I wonder if the kidnapper headed off to Canada or Mexico to escape getting caught." Elaine replies, "that is a good possibility, I guess anything is possible."

Once they finish eating lunch, Jane returns and asks, "will there be anything else?" Elaine asks, "would you boys like a hot fudge sundae?" They both nod their heads and say yes. Elaine says, "make that 3 hot fudge sundaes." Jane answers, "I'll be right back with those." She then walks off.

A few minutes later, Jane returns with the hot fudge sundaes, hands them out at leaves Elaine the check. Elaine thanks Jane for everything then Jane walks off. They all start to eat their sundaes and Elaine looks at the check. Once they are finished eating, Elaine leaves some money on the table as a tip for Jane. She picks up the check and the they go to the cashier to pay for their food.

Back at Kyle Smith's house, Kyle is on the phone with the police. He tells them that he would like to make a confession about Buster's kidnapping. He tells them that he would like an officer to come to the house, and bring him to the station, then he will tell his story then.

Elaine and the boys return home. After they get out of the car, Elaine says, "o.k. you boys can go swimming at Josh and Tyler's house." Mark and Scott run into the house in about 2 seconds flat. Elaine thinks to herself, "wow, I never seen them move so fast before." She then walks in.

Just as Elaine is gift wrapping the present for Jackie, Mark and Scott walk down stairs wearing their swimsuits, sandals, and their shirts. Elaine yells for them to come over. When they get there, she says, "I need you guys to sign Jackie's birthday card, then you can go." They both sign and head out the door.

Mark and Scott get out and start towel whipping each other. They laugh and giggle as they hit each other.

The police show up at Kyle's house. Kyle walks out and the police officer asks him, "are you sure you want to do this?" Kyle answers him, "do I have red hair and freckles?" Kyle with the cop and gets in the car.

Mark and Scott are walking down the street and they see Kyle get in the police car. Mark asks, "did you see that Scott? Kyle got into a police, only this time without hand cuffs." Scott answers, yeah, last time that happened, he was being arrested." Mark says, "let's stay here until they leave." They then stop walking. The police car leaves and the boys resume walking.

On the way to Josh and Tyler's house Scott says, "I wonder what he did this time." Mark then replies, "you never know about him, for all we know, he could have smashed up some guy's car." Scott then adds, "maybe they'll put him in jail a few years this time."

They arrive at Josh and Tyler's house and find Josh and Tyler sitting on the front steps where they saw everything. Mark says to Josh, "what do you think the police are doing with Kyle this time?" Josh answers, "I don't know, but I think it's weird that he went peacefully and without handcuffs." Mark adds, "yeah, last time he was handcuffed and he kicked and screamed."

All 4 of the boys then walked in the back yard, went to the picnic table and sat down. First they took off their sandals, then their shirts, put on some sunscreen and jumped in the pool. It didn't take long for them to start rough housing. All the fun was just beginning. After some rough housing, the boys decide to do some cannon balls. They would get out of the pool and see who could cannon ball jump in the farthest. Josh wins again.

At the Deerfield Police station, Kyle is in the Sargent's office talking to Sargent Henderson. People outside the office can see Kyle in there talking. Knowing his past, they start to whisper among themselves.

Some are saying, "what has he done this time? It must be really bad if he's talking to Sargent Henderson."

A short while later, Kyle and Sargent Henderson walk out of his office. The whispering stops. Kyle and Sargent Henderson make their way to the front of the police station. Sargent Henderson orders two police officers to get in their squad cars and follow him. People watch as they see Kyle get in the back seat of Sargent Henderson's car and take off with the 2 cops following close behind.

People at the station begin to talk. One lady says, "I bet they're taking him to the county jail this time." One man says, "yeah that good for nothing punk. I remember him. He started a fight with my son just a week before he went to jail. Knocked out 2 of my son's teeth." One other man said, "yeah, he sure is a menace."

Back at the Hanson's house, the boys are enjoying their swimming. Joyce walks out side with a pitcher of lemon aid and 4 glasses filled with ice. The boys get out of the pool, sit in some lawn chairs and start to pour their lemon aid and drink. Josh says, "thanks mom, that was really nice of you." Joyce then replies, "I thought you boys might be thirsty, so I made that for you guys." She then walks back in the house.

The boys are enjoying their lemon aid and Josh says, "after a while, why don't we go back in the pool, and have the ultimate chicken fight contest. Tyler and myself against you two. Best 3 out of 5 wins the championship." Mark replies, "you're on." The boys continue drinking their lemon aid. They tell some jokes and have fun laughing at their jokes.

After the boys finish their lemon aid, they jump right back in the pool. Then they get ready for the best of 5 chicken fights. Scott gets up on Mark's shoulders and Tyler up on Josh's. They begin the first chicken fight. After a very tough battle, Scott wins the first round. Mark says, "good job little brother, just 2 more times and we're the champs."

Back in Aurora, Dan Fredrickson is sitting in his living room and talking to a close friend on the phone. The friend suddenly notices 3 Deerfield Police cars entering Aurora and says, "that's odd." Dan asks, "what's odd?" The friend answers, "3 cop cars from Deerfield just entered the city, one with a boy in it." Dan is certain they are looking for him, so he gets off the phone with the friend.

Dan calls for his wife Shirley. She just finished ironing some clothes in the laundry room, then walks upstairs to the living room. She asks, "what do you want Dan?" Realizing this could be the last time he sees her he answers, "I've decided to take Buster to the park." He grabs Buster's leash and adds, "we'll be back in a half hour." Dan dashes out the door with Buster and they both get in the car, and take off in a hurry.

Shirley is puzzled why he took off so sudden. He didn't even kiss her goodbye. She returns to the laundry room and starts one final load in the dryer and starts that up. Then she grabs the clothes she ironed and folded. She brings them upstairs and puts them away. The doorbell rings and Shirley goes to answer it.

Shirley is stunned to see the police there with 3 squad cars. She asks, "can I help you?" Sargent Henderson asks, "do you have a German Shepard named Buster?" Shirley is even more puzzled. She is even afraid to answer the question, because she has a guess that they are looking for her dog.

Shirley slowly starts to cry, and wonders how Dan could have done this to her. She then answers, "I received Buster 2 or 3 weeks ago as an anniversary gift from my husband." Sargent Henderson says, "that is about the time we received a report back in Deerfield about a German Shepard named Buster was kidnapped." Shirley thinks, "oh Dan how could you?"

Sargent Henderson continues, "we have a boy with us that claims he saw Buster around here." Shirley looks at the squad car parked in front of the house, and sees Kyle sitting in it. Then she says, "my husband just left for the park not too long ago, and he took Buster with him." Sargent Henderson asks Shirley to ride with them to find Dan. She gets out, locks up the house and gets in the backseat of the main squad car with Kyle.

Dan is sitting on a park bench with Buster sitting on the ground next to him. All seems well, and he hopes the police don't show up. He sees a crow flying about 20 feet over him. He thinks, "this can't be good." The crow then flies off in a southern direction.

Dan then notices the 3 squad cars pulling into the parking lot. He sees the cops, Kyle, and Shirley getting out of the cars. He gets off the bench and starts to run with Buster beside him. The cops, along with Shirley and Kyle chase after him. The 1st place Dan runs to is the bike trails, he thinks he can lose them there.

He comes to a 3-way fork in the trail and goes left. The police come to that same fork, look around and see nothing. They split up in 3 groups and search all 3 trails. Dan finds 3 bushes and decides to hide in there. He gets to rest there for a couple minutes before 1 of the cops show up. Buster barks a couple times and the cop spots him.

Dan is annoyed that Buster gave them away. He gets up and starts running. The cop that spotted him announced on his radio that he found them and where. He chases after him and the others follow. Dan then starts to think of another place to hide.

As Dan is running, he finds an unpaved walking trail and runs over there. He runs as fast as he can with Buster run right behind him. He comes upon an open area and takes a quick look around. He sees 5 unpaved walking trails and he chooses the one that is hardest to see. He runs as fast as he can, hoping the cops will go in the wrong one.

When Dan reaches the end of trail, he comes up on an old abandoned house. The house is all boarded up, but the front door is open a crack. He manages to open the door and walks in. He walks in the living room and sees blood stains on the floor. He walks upstairs to the master bedroom and hides in the walk in closet.

The cops finally make it to the open area, and they stop for a while. Looking around, they see the 5 unpaved walking trails. Sargent Henderson declares, "well, we lost him, we'll never find him now." Kyle rolls his eyes and says, "don't be too sure of that Sargent, I know exactly where he went. He went down that (points to the hard to see trail) trail over there."

Everyone looks surprised how confident Kyle is when he points out that trail. Sargent Henderson asks, "how can you be sure?" Kyle looks him in eye and answers, "trust me, I know what I'm talking about, and in a few minutes, you'll see why." They all start off down that trail. With Kyle leading the way, they talk amongst themselves on how Kyle can be so sure of himself.

Kyle leads them right to the front door of the abandoned house. He then turns and faces everyone and says, "we must be quiet when we enter, we don't want to scare him and make him run." He turns facing the door, and enters in with the others following him.

They walk into the living room and Sargent Henderson notices the blood stains on the floor. Talking in a soft voice, he asks, "why are there blood stains on the floor?" Speaking softly, Kyle answers, "back when I was getting in trouble in school, you know, before I went to jail, I came across this house by accident. I snuck in and found out that a bunch of bad boys would hide here from the cops. They would be gambling at times hold fighting competitions here."

Sargent Henderson then asked, "did you fight or gamble here?" Kyle then answers, "hell yeah, I gambled at the kitchen table, and then later us guys would take our shirts off and hold our fighting competition here. I've been in 3 fights and won them all. In fact, (points to a blood stain) I caused a boy to bleed there."

Sargent Henderson then asked, "if you live in Deerfield, how did you end up here?" Kyle answers, "I have a grandma that lives in Aurora. Every once in a while, my parents would make me spend the weekend with her." Thinking that he heard enough, Sargent Henderson says, "o.k. let's break up in 2 groups and search for Dan. Kyle, you come up with me upstairs. You 2 guys look around here with Shirley and let's see if we can find him."

Kyle and Sargent Henderson start walking upstairs. Then Kyle says, "now remember Sargent that I told you that some bad kids hang out here when hiding from the cops. You might want to report that to the Aurora police." Sargent Henderson replies, "you beter believe that I will."

Back on the main level, Shirley and the 2 cops start their search for Dan. They walk through a hallway and find a bathroom on the right. They look in the shower and find nothing. They check the storage space under the sink, still nothing. All along, Shirley is hoping that once Dan is found that nothing happens that will cause him to get shot.

They leave the bathroom and head down the hallway. Next they walk into a family room. They walk up to this big closet, open the door and a bunch of dust falls. On the floor of the closet, they find an old phonograph from around the 1940's. Shirley says, "I wonder if it still works." On the top shelf, they find a collection of old newspapers that were from the 1940's as well. Shirley closes the door and they continue searching.

When Kyle and Sargent Henderson reach the top of the stairs, they decide to check the master bathroom first. Kyle slides the old shower curtain over first and finds nothing. Sargent Henderson opens the door to the linin closet and finds that empty. They leave the bathroom and move to a bedroom at the end of the hallway.

They walk in the bedroom and take a look in the closet. All they find in there is an old wedding gown on a hanger. Kyle thinks to himself, "what sort of people lived here?" They go in the bedroom next door. Sargent Henderson opens the closet door in that room. He finds a can of red spray paint and the word KILL spray painted on the back wall. Kyle looks at what Sargent Henderson found and says, "oh that's Andy Ericson's work. He was practicing for a vandalizing job he was going to do.

Kyle and Sargent Henderson look at each other and realize there is only one place left to look. Kyle is starting to worry that he could be wrong. This is something he has never been wrong about.

They walk in the master bedroom very quietly. Kyle steps on a board that creeks a little. He stops walking for a moment, then tries to be quieter. They get standing in front of the closet door. Sargent Henderson whispers to Kyle, "go stand over there, (points to a place just off to the side) you'll be safer if he runs for it, or starts shooting." Kyle does as he is asked.

Sargent Henderson draws out his gun and opens the door. He sees Dan and Buster in there, then yells, "freeze!" Dan knowing that he's caught, releases Buster and puts his hands up. Buster walks out of the closet and goes over to where Kyle is standing. Sargent Henderson gets on his radio and asks for the other 2 cops and Shirley to come upstairs.

Sargent Henderson grabs his handcuffs and slaps them on Dan's wrists. Just as Sargent Henderson is reading Dan his rights, Shirley and the other 2 cops enter the room. When Shirley sees Dan has been arrested, she cries out, "oh Dan how could you?" As Shirley stands before him, Dan remains silent as Shirley begins to cry.

The cops help Dan to his feet. One of the cops' hands Shirley a handkerchief to wipe the tears from her eyes. All Kyle can think about is how this time he isn't the one being arrested. Sargent Henderson looks at Kyle and says, "I don't know how yet, but when we get back to the police station, I'll find some way to reward you for your help." Kyle smiles as they all leave the room.

Back at the Hanson's house, the boys are playing around the pool. Joyce walks out to the pool and says, "Josh and Tyler, may I talk to you guys for a moment?" The boys stop their playing for a while and Joyce continues, "I got a call from your father. He got a call at work from

Deerfield Police. They're in Aurora going after some guy they think kidnapped Buster."

All 4 of the boys get excited when they hear this. Joyce continues, "David is on his way home now, and the Deerfield police maybe coming over as well to bring Buster home." All 4 of the boys high five one another as Joyce returns in the house. Then the boys go crazy in the pool.

After a few minutes going crazy in the pool Josh says, "what a day it's been. First Kyle gets picked up by the police, then the news that someone may have found Buster." Mark then adds, "that sure is making it for a busy day for Deerfield police." Josh thinks for a moment and says, I wonder who reported finding Buster to the police?"

David returns home sometime later. He sees the boys playing in the pool and decides to go talk to them. He walks in the back yard and Josh hollers to him, "dad!" The boys get out of the pool and dry off. They sit down at the picnic table and David walks up to them.

Looking at the boys, David says, "I guess you guys have heard the good news." Josh replies, "yeah mom told us." David nods his head and says, "yeah, I thought she would." Joyce and Kimberly walk out and greet David. Joyce then tells everyone that the police will be arriving soon.

A couple minutes later, 3 cop cars show up. The first has Sargent Henderson with Kyle and Buster in the back seat. The 2nd car has one the cops with Dan in the back seat in handcuffs. The 3rd is driven by the other cop. Then last, Shirley is seen driving her and Dan's car.

Everyone is puzzled to see a man they don't know in handcuffs and not Kyle. They all run toward the cars, just as the cops get out.

Sargent Henderson then announces, "I'm looking for a David and Joyce Hanson." David answers, "I'm David and this (points to Joyce) is my wife Joyce." They all walk a little closer to the cops, and Sargent Henderson says, "I'm Sargent Henderson of the Deerfield Police department." David and Sargent Henderson shake hands.

Sargent Henderson then signals Kyle and Buster to get out of his car. When they get out, Kimberly yells, "Buster!" All the kids run toward Buster and Kimberly gets there first. She hugs him and the other kids hug and pets him. Kyle backs off a few feet and watches.

David and Joyce are pleased to see how the kids react to the return of Buster. They both get into wondering, who to thank for this? Sargent

Henderson explains, "you can thank Kyle Smith for this. He's the real hero." Everyone stops what they're doing, looks at Kyle with shock in their faces. Then David points to Kyle and asks, "what? Him?"

Nobody can believe what they just heard. Then David says, "that's the kid that beats up the other kids in the neighborhood and takes their lunch money." Sargent Henderson replies, "believe it or not, he's the one who came to the police office, sat in my office and told me everything. He even lead us to an abandoned house where we found Dan Fredrickson and Buster hiding."

Joyce takes a good look at Kyle and wonders how he knew so much. Considering the fact that he didn't have very good grades in school, made things even more interesting that he is the one who found Buster. Kyle then looks back at everyone with a big grin on his face. Then he thinks to himself, "cool, now here is my chance to score some points with everyone."

Joyce then asks, "well Kyle, will you please tell us how you knew so much?" Kyle's grin gets a little bigger, then he answers, "sure. It all started one day when I was visiting my grandma in Aurora. I went to the local park there to play. I saw a strange man and Buster walk in the park. Something didn't look right, so I hid myself behind some bushes and spied on the man."

Kyle continues his story, "when he got off the park bench, I watched where he went. I heard some lady call for Buster and I knew this guy was the one you might be looking for. I got up and ran after him, keeping myself hidden as best I could. I followed him to his house and made a mental note of the address. Then wrote that address down a slip of paper when I got back to my grandma's house. I've kept that paper in my pocket ever since."

After hearing Kyle's story Joyce asks, "if you knew so much then, why didn't you tell us or the police when you got home?" Kyle then replies, "I thought about that, then realized, nobody would believe me, after all I lied to you all a lot and everyone had a bit of a dislike toward me. I don't blame you, with the way I behaved over the last couple of years, and for that, I'm sorry."

Sargent Henderson then adds, "that's a great story Kyle, but there is one thing that saddens me. Buster was an anniversary gift from Dan to his wife Shirley. It's sad she must lose her gift, but Buster does belong to you. Everyone feels saddened that Shirley has lost her gift.

Knowing what Buster must have meant to Shirley, David announces, "I may be able to remedy this problem. Just let me make a phone call." David then gets out his cell phone and makes a call.

When David is done with his call, he announces he has good news for Shirley. He walks up to her car and asks her to roll down her window. She does and David says to her, "I know that you loved Buster, and I'd hate to see you leave empty handed. I have a friend that works at a near by pound. He has a German Shepard that is a lot like Buster, he said you can have him for free.

Shirley stops crying and stats to smile. David gets out a business card from his wallet and hands it to Shirley and says, "here's his business card of his, just go to this address, he'll be expecting you." Shirley thanks David, looks at the card and drives off. David then walks back to where Joyce is standing.

Sargent Henderson and the other cops say goodbye to everyone and get in their cars. As they leave, everyone waves goodbye to the cops. Dan has a very sad look on his face, because he is now on his way to jail.

David calls for Kyle to come over. Kyle walks over to where David and Joyce are standing. David says to Kyle, "I'll make arrangements with your parents for that $500 reward for Buster, you earned it." Kyle smiles really big and says, "thanks!"

Joyce then says, "you wanted to swim in our pool when we had a private pool party. I said no then, but now I think you earned it." Kyle replies, "I had a feeling you'd say that. I was wearing my swimsuit under my shorts just in case." Kyle then takes off his shirt, shorts, and shoes leaving just his swimsuit on. He takes his clothes and runs in the back yard. He places his clothes on the picnic table, then runs and jumps in the pool.

Printed in the United States
By Bookmasters